Oh, Buoy!

Collect all the books in the Luna Bay *series*

*coming soon

Luna Bay

a ROXY GiRL series

BOOK FOUR

Oh, Buoy!

by Francess Lantz

Win
a Roxy Girl
Shopping Spree
at ROXY.com
see details in back

HarperEntertainment
An Imprint of HarperCollinsPublishers

LUNA BAY: OH, BUOY! Copyright © 2003 by Quiksilver, Inc. All rights reserved. Printed in the United States of America. No part of this book may be used or reproduced in any manner whatsoever without written permission except in the case of brief quotations embodied in critical articles and reviews. For information address HarperCollins Publishers Inc., 10 East 53rd Street, New York, NY 10022.

HarperCollins books may be purchased for educational, business, or sales promotional use. For information please write: Special Markets Department, HarperCollins Publishers Inc., 10 East 53rd Street, New York, NY 10022.

FIRST EDITION

Designed by Jackie McKee

ISBN 0-06-057373-2

WBC/RRD 10 9 8 7 6 5 4 3 2 1

For my surf posse:
Carol Vandenberg, Michael Petracca,
and Bruce Hale

Acknowledgments

With thanks to Elvia Lopez, Rob Colby,
Stan Witnov, John Landsberg, Jodie Ireland,
Jeffery McGraw, Matt Jacobson, Danielle Beck,
and Kendra Marcus.

I don't see a parking space, Papi," Isobel says as her father steers the car into the crowded dirt parking lot above Carson Beach. "Why don't you just drop me off? I'll call you later if I need a ride."

"Wait," her father says, swerving to miss some kids in Crescent Cove High School sweatshirts, "I think I see one!"

"The dust is terrible," Isobel's mother mutters. "The car is going to be filthy by the end of the day."

Isobel rolls her eyes. Her mother is totally obsessed with keeping the car clean. She's the same way with the house. Everything has to be spotless or she freaks. Isobel thinks it's silly, but right now she isn't complaining. Maybe Mami's obsession can be used to her advantage.

"It's pretty windy today," Isobel says. "If it's dusty here, just think what the beach is going to be like.

Sand blowing in your face, the bright sun in your eyes . . ."

But Mami doesn't get the hint. "What do you think of this hat?" she asks, turning around to model a straw hat with a wide brim. "Very California, don't you think?"

Isobel and her family moved to Crescent Cove from Denver, Colorado, a little over a year ago. To Isobel's embarrassment, Mami and Papi still think anything Californian is novel and noteworthy. Not that Isobel feels totally at home. Last year she was snowboarding in the Rockies; this year she's surfing in the Pacific. It's a big change, and sometimes she feels like a visitor in a strange land. Still, she doesn't feel the need to broadcast her culture shock to the entire world.

"Can we bring our Game Boys to the beach?" Isobel's ten-year-old brother Miguel pipes up.

"Please?" his twin brother, Toni, pleads.

"No, *mi hijos*," Mami scolds. "If they get sand in them, they'll be ruined."

The boys let out a groan, and Isobel tries one more time. "The boys are going to be bored. Why don't you just drop me off and—"

"Isobel," her father breaks in, "we don't want to drop you off. This is your first surf meet, and we're here to support you. A few minor inconveniences aren't going to stop us."

Isobel feels a pang of guilt. Why is she trying so hard to get rid of her family? They're here because they love her, she knows that. And she loves them, too.

It's just that sometimes their attention feels like a wet suit that's two sizes too tight. She longs to peel it off and swim free.

Isobel's father pulls into a parking space next to a school bus with the words SANTA BARBARA SCHOOL DISTRICT on the side. Isobel watches as a trio of girls walks off the bus. She recognizes one of them, a tall blonde with a face and body straight out of a *Sports Illustrated* swimsuit issue. It's Vanessa Haddix, one of the best teenage surfers around. Three of Isobel's best friends, Luna, Rae, and Cricket, surfed against Vanessa in the ASA Western Championship at the beginning of the summer. Vanessa beat them all.

Will she do it again this weekend? Isobel wonders.

Miguel and Toni burst out of the backseat and clamor down the stairs that lead to the beach. Isobel unstraps her board from the top of the car and follows them. Her parents bring up the rear, their arms loaded with towels, sunscreen, and coolers full of food.

The beach is crowded with kids, parents, and dogs. Under a tent with a sign that reads CRESCENT COVE HIGH SCHOOL, Isobel finds her best friends and teammates, Luna, Rae, Cricket, and Kanani.

"What took you so long?" Luna asks. She's sitting in the sand, stretching her torso over her long, willowy legs. "The first heat starts in fifteen minutes."

"Miguel couldn't find his Game Boy," Isobel replies with a shrug. "Then my dad had to stop by the new store."

3

Isobel's father owns a chain of sportswear stores. He opened the first one in Denver, Colorado, almost twenty years ago, and last year he opened his fifth store in the new mall on the I5.

Cricket holds up her breakfast—a package of chocolate doughnuts. "Want one?" she asks.

Isobel shakes her head. It's so unfair. Cricket seems to live on a diet of junk food, yet she's rail thin and full of energy. *If I ate like that, I'd weigh two hundred pounds*, Isobel thinks with an inward groan.

Rae looks up from waxing her surfboard. She's got three tiny braids in her short, strawberry-blonde locks, each with a blue bead dangling at the bottom.

"I like your hair," Isobel says. "When did you do that?"

"Luna did it. She slept over last night." She squints out at the ocean. Wind-whipped four-foot waves are rolling in. "You ready to charge it?"

Isobel nods. "Did you know Vanessa Haddix is here?"

The girls look startled. Then Luna says, "She's from Santa Barbara. We should have figured she'd be on the high school team."

"I thought she was going pro," Kanani remarks, pulling her thick, dark hair back into a ponytail.

"That's next year, after she graduates," Luna says.

Cricket chomps on a doughnut. "Oh, man, she's too good," she mumbles.

"Don't say that," Luna counters. "She's not invincible."

"I can beat her," Rae declares. "Just watch me!"

Isobel admires Rae's aggro attitude. When it comes to competition, she's like a hungry shark—relentless, fearless.

Isobel wonders if she'll ever be like that. She loves to surf, but contests just don't excite her that much. There are too many rules, too much sitting around and waiting, too much showing off. What thrills her is going one-on-one with a big wave—dropping down the face, racing the curl, flying over the back before it closes out and crushes her.

"Hey, look," Cricket says, "they're posting the heats."

The girls hurry over to check it out. The boys on the team surf first—three heats of four surfers each, two from each school. Then it's the girls' turn. Isobel and Cricket go up against Vanessa and another SBHS girl, Daisy Gingras, in the first heat. Rae and Kanani surf in the next heat, and Luna and another CCHS girl, Maddie Pillsbury, are in the last heat.

Isobel swallows hard. Can she hold her own against Vanessa? Only time will tell.

"Isobel?" her mother calls. "Come here, dear."

Isobel's parents have spread out their towel next to Luna's mom and dad. Looking at them, Isobel can't help but notice the difference in the two couples. Luna's parents, Tuck and Cate, are both surfers, and they look it. They're tan and fit, dressed in bathing suits and rash guards. Isobel's parents, on the other hand, are in long pants and long-sleeve shirts. Mami wears her straw hat, and Papi sports a khaki fishing cap.

Isobel winces. They look like they belong back in Denver, not on a beach in southern California.

"Explain the contest to your brothers," Mami says. "How does the judging work?"

"We surf in heats of four girls each," Isobel begins. "The preliminary heats are this morning, the semifinals are this afternoon. The finals are—"

But Miguel and Toni are too busy shoving each other to listen. Suddenly, Toni grabs a handful of sand and flings it at his brother.

"Boys!" Papi cries. "Stop that!"

Miguel gives Toni a final shove and then asks, "What's going on over there?" He points to a tent decorated with surf company logos—Edge SurfWear, Chunky Surf Wax, Bali Boards, Wave Star Surf Systems. A group of kids—some little, some teenagers—are standing on soft-top surfboards while three older kids instruct them.

"Looks like a clinic," Isobel says. "The companies hand out free stickers, give kids surf tips, stuff like that. Why don't you check it out?"

The boys dash to the tent, and Isobel's mother smiles, pleased that Isobel has distracted them from fighting. "When do you surf, Isobel?"

"Not for a while. The boys' team goes first."

"Sit down. Have a snack."

But Isobel doesn't want to hang out with her parents now. She's too edgy, too hyped up. If she starts eating, she'll probably scarf down an entire bag of chips.

"Later," she says. "I'm going for a walk until my heat starts."

She heads up the beach in the direction of the clinic tent. As she gets closer, she hears a male voice speaking fluent Spanish.

"*Bien. Cuando sientas la ola empujarte, brinca a tus pies.*"

Isobel pauses, wondering who among the surfers speaks Spanish. She's surprised to see it's a teenager with shiny red hair, blue eyes, and freckles.

He certainly doesn't look Latino, she thinks. *So where did he learn to speak Spanish like that?*

The teen turns to a skinny girl, probably no more than six years old. She tries to jump up on the surfboard, but instead she catches her foot and trips. The boy on the next surfboard snickers.

"Hey, dude," the redheaded boy says seriously, "I wouldn't laugh if I were you. One day soon this little girl is going to be out there ripping. You get on her bad side, she might snake your waves."

Isobel giggles. She likes the way this guy relates to the kids. He's relaxed, he's funny, and he doesn't talk down to them.

She watches as he turns back to the boy on his left. "*Trátalo otra vez. Y después saldremos al mar.*"

Isobel sighs. There's something else she likes about

this guy—he's a total hottie! He's got wide, muscular shoulders, a washboard stomach, and strong, tree trunk legs. His thick hair curls over his ears and down his neck. And his smile makes even the most uncoordinated grommet feel at ease.

Isobel can't help but wonder what it would feel like to have that smile aimed at her. But she knows she'll never find out. She doesn't know this guy, and she certainly isn't about to walk up and introduce herself. What would she say? What would she do with her hands? What if she froze up, or stuttered, or said something totally stupid? She'd die of embarrassment.

Besides, she reminds herself, boys aren't interested in Isobel Rodriguez. Her shoulders are too broad, her legs are too short, her stomach isn't flat enough. Her face is okay, she supposes, but nothing special. All right, so her girlfriends are always telling her how amazing her long black hair is. And yes, the hennaed highlights she put in last weekend look pretty good. But nice hair just isn't enough to get a boy interested in her. At least, it hasn't been so far.

"*Adiós, guapísimo*," she whispers wistfully. *So long, handsome.* Then she turns and walks away.

When the air horn blows to announce the beginning of the heat, Isobel throws her board in the water and paddles hard. Soon she's sitting in the lineup with Cricket, Vanessa, and Daisy. Cricket, never known for her patience, takes the first wave and shreds it at warp speed. Vanessa takes the next wave. Isobel watches as she flies off the lip and lands a perfect 180.

Whoa, Isobel thinks, *that girl is good!*

Next is the set wave, a solid five-footer. Daisy paddles for it, but Isobel is in position. She drops into a power turn, sails across the face, and disappears into the tube. It closes out before she can emerge, but it still feels like a pretty good first ride.

As she paddles back out, she notices a male surfer paddling outside the lineup. He's moving fast, just paddling for exercise it seems. Then she realizes it's *him*—the boy from the surf clinic!

"See that guy?" she calls to Cricket.

"Yeah?" she answers, only half looking. Her eyes are focused on the waves.

"Do you know who he is?" Isobel persists.

Vanessa, floating a few yards away, answers. "His name is Roger Copenhaver. Why?"

Isobel doesn't know what to say. She's not about to tell Vanessa Haddix she's got the hots for this guy—what's his name?—Roger Copen-something. That's the sort of information she would share only with her closest friends. But then what *should* she say?

Finally, she takes the easy way out and catches the next wave that comes along. Fortunately, it's a beauty. She charges across the face, pulls off a big roundhouse cutback, then floats over the whitewater to make the inside section.

Isobel manages one more long ride before the final

horn sounds. Paddling in, she can't help grinning. She performed well, she knows it. But was it good enough to make it to the semis? She isn't sure.

Luna, Rae, and Kanani are waiting on the shore. "Isobel, you were on fire!" Rae shouts.

"Hey, what about me?" Cricket asks.

"You ripped," Luna says. "But I think you should have held out for better waves."

"I was distracted," Cricket complains. "Isobel was talking to me about some boy who was paddling outside the lineup."

All heads snap in Isobel's direction. "Some boy, huh?" Kanani says with a grin.

Isobel shrugs with embarrassment. "His name is Roger; that's all I know," she confesses. "I saw him teaching at the surf clinic. He was great with the kids, and he speaks Spanish, and well . . . he's hot!"

"Then you've got to talk to him," Luna says matter-of-factly.

"I can't. I mean, what would I say?"

"Say *'Boy, you rock my world!'* " Rae sings in her most soulful voice.

The girls dissolve into giggles. Then suddenly, Cricket whispers, "Don't look now, but here he comes!"

Of course, everyone looks—everyone except Isobel, who can feel her cheeks burning. Panicking, she drops her board and practically runs toward her parents.

"Isobel," her father calls, jumping to his feet, "you looked sensational out there!"

Mami hugs Isobel and kisses her cheeks. "That's my girl!"

"Mami, please," Isobel mutters, pulling away. Why does her mother have to slobber all over her in public?

She grabs a Gatorade from the cooler and hurries over to the judges' tent. One of the judges is posting the heat results. With her heart pounding, Isobel looks over the man's shoulder. A gasp escapes her lips. Both she and Vanessa made it to the semifinals!

Isobel steps back and finds herself surrounded by Luna, Rae, Cricket, and Kanani. "I—I made it!" she stutters.

They all hug her, even Cricket, and her heart overflows with love for her incredible friends. What would she do without them?

Then she looks up and—oh, my gosh—there he is again! Roger, handsome Roger, in his surf trunks and Wave Star tank top, is walking by, so close she could almost touch him. Suddenly, she can't think, she can't move, she can't even breathe.

"Talk to him," Rae whispers.

She shakes her head vehemently.

"Go for it," Luna urges. "Just ask him the time or something."

"Go on!" Cricket hisses, giving Isobel a shove.

Isobel stumbles forward and loses her balance. Suddenly, everything switches into slow motion. She falls into Roger with the force of a linebacker. He hits the sand with a thud, and she collapses on top of him.

Instantly, the world shifts to fast forward. Isobel leaps to her feet. In a squeaky cartoon voice she cries, "Oh! I—I—I'm sorry!"

Roger looks up at her and frowns. "Yeah, me, too."

Isobel wants to dig a hole in the sand and crawl into it. Why in the world did Cricket have to shove her? She could just strangle that girl.

Roger gets to his feet. Now he's smiling. "Are you competing today?"

Isobel's mouth is as dry as Death Valley in August. She can't possibly form words, so she just nods.

"Well, if you move with as much power in the water as you do on land, you must be one awesome surfer."

Isobel wants to say something clever and witty, but her mind is on permanent delete. Like an idiot, she just stands there.

Finally, when it becomes obvious to Roger that she's either a deaf mute or an imbecile, he backs away. "Well, have a good one," he mutters as he wanders off into the crowd and—Isobel is quite certain—out of her life forever.

2

*I*sobel is asleep, dreaming about dropping in. It's her favorite part of surfing. She loves feeling a big wave rise up beneath her, then paddling hard, so hard her muscles burn, until she feels herself dropping down, down, down a shimmering gray-green wall of water.

In her dream, Isobel looks down and tenses. Someone has already taken off on the wave, and she's about to drop in on him. She tries to pull out, but it's too late. She hears a crack, then feels flesh slam against flesh.

She dives underwater and opens her eyes. And then she sees him. It's Roger, and he's looking at her, too. "Are you all right?" he asks, his voice clear and crisp.

But when Isobel tries to answer, water fills her mouth. All she can manage is a choking, blubbering sound. And now she's gulping in water, gasping for air, going down . . . down . . .

A sharp, high-pitched wail jars her from her dream. She leaps up, heart pounding, only to realize it's the phone. With a groan, she answers it.

"Isobel, is that you?" asks Cricket. "Come on, I'm sorry about yesterday. Answer me, will you?"

"Hey," Isobel mutters groggily, "I just had the weirdest dream—"

"Well, wake up to reality, *chica*!" Cricket interrupts in her usual mile-a-minute way. "I checked the online surf reports, and it's pumping out there. I mean, head-high with an occasional eight-footer."

Isobel is instantly wide awake. "For real? Are you sure it said Carson Beach?"

"It's the entire south coast. So rise and shine and get ready to blow Santa Barbara High out of the water." Then, without so much as a good-bye, she hangs up.

Isobel flops back on her bed. It's moments like this when she wishes she could live where her friend Luna lives—just a few blocks from the ocean in a two-story house with an unobstructed view of the surf. Instead, she lives in a new development in the hills. Here, the only view is of houses, houses, and more houses.

Still, she can use her imagination. She closes her eyes and pictures head-high sets rolling into Carson Beach. She feels a shiver of anticipation, excitement, and anxiety all mixed together. It's the same way she used to feel when she went snowboarding in the Colorado backcountry. No groomed trails or crowded half-pipes for her, thank you. Her bliss was an empty mountain dotted with trees and rocks, dusted with a coating of fresh powder.

Isobel remembers how she panicked when her parents decided to move to Crescent Cove last year. The closest snow-covered mountain was a good six hours away. What was she going to do with herself? How would she survive? But her fears faded when she discovered surfing. She mastered the basics almost immediately, and soon she was ready for more—more size, more speed, more thrills.

Now, stretched out on her bed, Isobel smiles, thinking of what awaits her at the beach this morning. She can almost feel the burn in her muscles as she paddles for a big one, almost feel her heart leap into her throat as she drops in. "Carson Beach," she whispers as the first rays of morning sunshine slip across the floor, "here I come!"

"Ah, this is more like it," Isobel's father declares as he drives into the uncrowded Carson Beach parking lot.

"But where are the people?" her mother asks. "I thought the final heats were this morning."

"They are," Isobel answers, "but the fog is keeping most of the kids away. They'll show up later when it burns off."

Mami makes a *tsk-tsk* sound with her tongue. "You need your friends to cheer you on."

Isobel just shrugs. Miguel and Toni didn't come this morning either, but she doesn't care. It's the waves that interest her. As soon as Papi parks, she grabs her board and jogs to the stairs. "I'll meet you down at the beach," she calls.

At the top step, she stops and stares. She can't see much because of the fog, but what she *can* see gives her goose bumps. Huge walls of water are rolling out of the mist, rising and cresting until they crash with booming force in the shallow water. They look even bigger than Cricket predicted, but it's hard to tell until she sees someone riding.

"Ah, here comes my secret weapon," Coach Daily calls as Isobel arrives at the team tent. He looks up from his clipboard and smiles. "You ready for the big stuff?"

Suddenly, Isobel feels a pang of trepidation. Her coach is counting on her. Can she pull it off? "I'm ready to try," she says.

"Can't ask for more than that. And remember, you've been on waves almost this big before. Don't let them intimidate you. Just do what you always do, and you'll be fine."

Kanani appears behind Isobel. "I'm glad I didn't make it into the finals. I would have brought down our scores."

Kanani is a longboarder. Graceful nose-walking is what she does best. "We've all got our own style," Isobel says, and she means it. In fact, it's one of the things she loves about her friends. Luna is the best all-around surfer, Rae is the most aggressive, Kanani is the most graceful, and Cricket is the best ripper. But they all have one thing in common—they all surf as if their lives depended on it.

By the time the judges post the final heats, the rest of the team has arrived. Everyone runs over to check the list. The girls surf first today, in three one-on-one heats. Only Isobel, Rae, and Luna have made it to the finals.

"Look, Isobel," Rae says. "You're surfing first—against Vanessa Haddix!"

Isobel swallows hard, trying to ignore the butterflies in her stomach. If only she wasn't up against Vanessa—probably the best female amateur on the entire West Coast.

"Hey, no worries," Rae insists. "You're going to blow Fish Face out of the water."

"Fish Face?" Isobel repeats uncertainly.

"You know, Vanessa *Haddock*," Rae quips.

The girls groan and giggle. Isobel joins in, grateful for something to distract her from her precontest jitters. Returning to the team tent, she gets into her wet suit and waxes her board, all the while keeping an eye on the surf. There are a few surfers in the water now, and she can see the waves curling over their heads as they drop in.

Isobel's heart kicks into overdrive. She's never been in surf this big, and she doesn't know whether to be elated or scared silly. But when her mother enters the tent and offers her a Gatorade and asks, "Are you sure you're ready for this, *mi hija*?" she waves her off. She's never been more ready. She's sure of it.

Finally, it's time. Isobel grabs her board and runs to the water's edge. Vanessa steps up beside her. "Have you ever been on waves this big before?" she asks Isobel.

"No," Isobel answers honestly.

Vanessa just smiles. "Good luck."

Is she trying to intimidate me? Isobel wonders. She looks out at the waves. Standing at water level, they look even bigger than they did from the team tent. A gnawing uncertainty grips her. Can she beat Vanessa? Can she even come close?

She's still wondering when the air horn blasts through the moist morning air. Isobel throws herself into the surf and paddles hard through the thundering whitewater. To her amazement, she beats Vanessa to the lineup. On the horizon, a sweet set is rolling in. She lets the first wave pass under her. Then, just as Vanessa paddles up beside her, she takes off on a huge wall of water.

Her mind is a total blank as the wave rises beneath her. She's just a machine with robot arms churning through the water. Then suddenly she starts falling and her brain switches to hyper-alert mode. She leans into a big bottom turn and roars across the open face, sending up a rooster tail of whitewater. Everything is crisp and clear and beautiful. She heads for the lip, cuts back hard, and finds the pocket. She's flying!

When the wave closes out, she shoots over the back and lets out a triumphant whoop. She glances toward shore and sees her teammates jumping up and down. *How big was that wave?* she wonders. Overhead, for sure, maybe bigger. And she conquered it!

As she paddles back out, she's almost surprised to see Vanessa taking off on a wave. She had actually forgotten they were competing against each other. All that mattered was making the wave. And all that matters now is catching another wave and doing it again.

The next fifteen minutes pass in a flash. When the horn sounds to signal the end of the heat, Isobel can't believe it. She doesn't want to go in. As she paddles reluctantly toward shore, she tries to remember how many waves she caught. Four? Five? And what about Vanessa? Did she catch her three required waves? Isobel didn't even notice.

And now, for the first time since the heat began, she wonders, *Did I do okay? Did I win?*

She knows the answer as soon as she reaches the shorebreak. Her team and her coach are waiting in the shallows, their faces glowing. As she splashes out of the water, they gather around her.

"You were awesome!" Luna cries. "Unreal!"

"Where did you learn to surf like that?" Coach Daily asks.

"On the slopes of the Rockies," Isobel replies. Everyone laughs, but she knows it's true. She surfed today the same way she snowboards—all-out.

The girls head back to the team tent, but Isobel is intercepted by her parents. "You looked beautiful out there!" Papi exclaims, hugging her tight. "How do you feel?"

"Like I want to do it again," she answers.

"My daughter, the California surfer." Mami chuckles. Then she frowns. "You look tired. Come, sit down and rest."

But Isobel shakes her head. That's the last thing she feels like doing now. "Later," she says. "Luna's heat is about to start. I want to cheer her on."

"We won! We won!" Cricket shouts. "Crescent Cove rules!"

Isobel reads the final results again, hardly daring to believe her eyes. It's no surprise to her that Luna and Rae won their heats. But what's amazing is that she beat Vanessa—*and* racked up the highest score of all the girls.

"Isobel, you totally rock!" Luna cries.

"I told you you'd smoke Vanessa," Rae proclaims. "Was I right or what?"

"The bigger the wave, the better you surf," Kanani says with awe in her voice. "How do you do that?"

"I don't know," Isobel answers truthfully. "I see

those big waves rolling in, and I just get pumped. All I want to do is charge them."

"Vanessa must be steaming." Cricket giggles. "She thinks she's unbeatable."

"Guess we showed her," Rae says with a cocky smile.

"Hey, the boys' heats are starting," Luna announces. "Let's go show our support."

The girls hurry over to join Coach Daily and the rest of the team under the tent. But Isobel hangs back, gazing one more time at the final scores. "I beat Vanessa Haddix," she whispers, as a grin spreads up her cheeks. Suddenly, contests don't seem so stupid after all. Not when they turn out like this one!

"Nice job," says a deep voice behind her.

Isobel spins around to find Roger reading the results over her shoulder. Instantly, her knees go weak, and her tongue turns to rubber. "Uh, th-thanks," she stutters.

"I was watching you," he says, flipping his red hair off his forehead. "You looked really good out there—strong, confident, focused, the whole package. How long have your been surfing?"

Speak! Isobel commands her brain. "Um, a little over a year."

"No way! Have you entered any ASA contests?"

She shakes her head.

"Well, you must have a sponsor, right?"

Is he kidding? She's never even dreamed of something like that. She shakes her head again.

"Isobel Rodriguez," he says, reading her name off

the result listings. "Guess I'd better remember that name. I'm pretty sure I'm going to be hearing it a lot in the next couple of years."

Isobel giggles stupidly. But instead of rolling his eyes and walking away, Roger says, "You're probably thinking, Who is this fool? My name is Roger Copenhaver. I've been helping out with the kids' clinic."

He holds out his hand, and Isobel shakes it, certain her palm must be dripping with sweat. But if it is, he doesn't seem to notice. Instead he says, "I hear they're having a party at one of the local restaurants after the contest."

Isobel manages a nod. "The Beachside Grill," she says.

"Yeah, that's it. Are you going?"

"I—I guess so," she answers.

He smiles, and his eyes crinkle up in a way that makes Isobel's skin tingle. "I was hoping you'd say that," he replies. "I'll see you there then."

With that, he walks away, leaving Isobel with her mouth hanging open and her heart dancing for joy.

3

*M*ake way for the winner!" Rae shouts as the Crescent Cove High School surf team presses toward the doors leading to the Beachside Grill's outdoor patio.

Everyone stops and moves aside, and Isobel finds herself walking through the door alone, like a princess entering her throne room. She grins foolishly and mutters, "Stop it, guys," but inside she's beaming. She's never won a contest before. She's never won *anything* before. It feels good.

But winning isn't the only thing on her mind. Roger is coming to the party. *Is he here yet?* she wonders, glancing around the patio. *Is he looking at me?* She feels instantly self-conscious and reaches up to run her hands through her salty, sandy hair. Oh, why hadn't she gone home and washed it?

She knows the answer. The girls wanted to stay and support the boys' team, and that left no time for anything except rushing to the restaurant. Besides, this is supposed to be an informal get-together. Everyone is sandy and windblown, and it doesn't matter.

Everyone, that is, except Vanessa Haddix. She's sitting at a table with her teammates, looking as if she just walked out of a day spa. Every hair is in place, her lips are glossy, her cheeks are glowing. Plus, unlike the other girls, who are wearing their bathing suits with T-shirts and shorts pulled on over them, Vanessa is wearing a short skirt and a turquoise long-sleeved blouse.

Isobel sits down with the girls' team. She's ordering fish tacos and lemonade when she sees Roger walk in with two other surfers from the surf clinic. Instantly, her heart shifts into overdrive. Will he wave to her? Walk over?

But no, he doesn't even look her way. Instead, he sits next to Coach Daily and reaches for a tortilla chip. Isobel slumps down in her chair. She doesn't know whether to feel disappointed or relieved.

"Isn't that the guy . . . ?" Cricket begins.

"What's your plan this time, Cricket?" Kanani teases. "Are you going to trip Isobel when she walks by his table?"

"You'd better not!" Isobel cries.

"He *is* kind of hot," Rae muses. "A little too pumped up for my taste, but still . . ."

"Rae, I thought you were going out with that lifeguard from Sola Beach," Cricket says.

Rae shrugs. "I am, but I can look, can't I?"

"No!" Luna answers. "This is the first guy I've ever seen Isobel drool over. She's got dibs on him."

"I'm not drooling." Isobel giggles. "Well, not so you'd notice, anyway."

"Oh, yeah, right," Kanani says with a snort. "Here's Isobel when he walked in." She chomps on a chip and gapes in Roger's direction. The half-chewed chip dribbles out of her mouth. The girls crack up.

"Stop it!" Isobel protests, giggling.

Just then, the boys from the CCHS surf team walk up to the table. "Anybody feel like dancing?" Jed Karlek asks, pointing to the tiny dance floor in the corner of the restaurant.

The sound system is pumping out Christina Aguilera's latest hit. "Sure," Luna says, jumping to her feet. Rae and Kanani join her, but Cricket and Isobel stay behind.

"I can't dance," Cricket confides after they've left. "I'm like totally spastic."

Isobel laughs. She likes to dance in front of her mirror at home. Secretly, she thinks she's got some good moves. But in public? She'd be way too embarrassed.

"Me, too," she lies.

Now the Santa Barbara High surf teams gets up to join the Crescent Cove kids on the dance floor.

"Don't look now," Cricket hisses, "but guess who's coming over."

Isobel's head swivels around and she finds herself looking up at Roger.

"Hi," he says with a smile. "You want to dance?"

"No, thanks," she mutters, trying to ignore her somersaulting stomach.

"Then do you mind if I sit down?"

"Okay."

"I'm going to the rest room," Cricket announces, jumping up.

Suddenly, Isobel finds herself alone with Roger. For a long, painful moment, no one says anything. Then Roger clears his throat and asks, "What did you order?"

"Fish tacos."

"Ah, *tacos con pescado. Yo tambien.*"

Finally, Isobel has something to say! Eagerly, she asks, "How did you learn to speak such good Spanish?"

"How do you know I speak it well?" he asks. "All I said was *tacos con pescado*. I could have read that off a menu."

"I heard you speaking Spanish to a kid in the surf clinic," she admits.

"So you've been spying on me, huh?" he says teasingly.

She can feel her face grow hot. "No!"

Roger laughs. "My dad is a Spanish professor at UC Irvine. He's been speaking Spanish to me all my life. Plus, we spend a couple of weeks in Mexico every summer."

"So you live in Irvine?" Isobel asks.

"My parents do. I live in San Clemente. I'm going to junior college and working part-time."

Isobel feels her heart sink. Roger is a college student. Could he possibly be interested in a lowly high school student like her? Not very likely.

"Have you lived in Crescent Cove all your life?" he asks.

"Only a year. I grew up in Colorado."

"Let me guess," he says with a knowing smile. "You're a snowboarder."

"Practically since I learned to walk. But how—?"

"There had to be some explanation for why you learned to surf so well so fast." He reaches for a tortilla chip. "What's the biggest wave you've ever surfed, Isobel?"

"You saw it this morning."

"Seriously? Oh, man, that's just the tip of the iceberg. Have you ever been to the North Shore?"

She shakes her head.

"You've got to go. But first you need to practice on some really good California surf—Rincon, La Jolla Cove, breaks like that. Winter surf can be unpredictable, though. You have to check the Internet every day. When a big swell hits, you just hop in your car and go."

"I wish," Isobel says wistfully. "But there's no way my parents are going to let me skip school to go surfing. And on weekends I have to work at my father's store."

Roger looks at her thoughtfully. "What you need is a sponsor—someone to set up surf trips for you, enter you in the contests, pay for your gear. Sometimes they even give you a weekly stipend. Pretty cool, huh? You actually get paid to surf."

Isobel sighs. "It sounds like a dream come true," she says. But that's all it is—a dream. She's knows she's not good enough yet to attract a sponsor.

Just then, the waitresses show up with everyone's food. The girls come back from the dance floor, and Roger returns to his table.

"Now we know why Isobel didn't want to dance," Luna says with a grin.

"Come on, spill," Rae demands. "What's he like?"

Isobel thinks it over. To her amazement, she realizes she just talked to Roger for a whole ten minutes without getting hopelessly tongue-tied. After she stopped thinking about how handsome he was, it was a snap.

"He's easy to talk to," she says. "But he's not interested in me or anything. I mean, he's in junior college. I'm probably just a kid to him."

"He wasn't looking at you like he thought you were a kid," Kanani declares.

"Really?" But she can't quite believe it. Why would a hottie like Roger be interested in her?

The sound of a spoon being tapped against a glass grabs everyone's attention. The girls turn to see Coach Daily and the Santa Barbara coach getting to their feet.

"A toast to the winners," the Santa Barbara coach says. "Crescent Cove High School!" He hands a first-place trophy to Coach Daily.

"And to our top competitors," Coach Daily continues. "Jed Karlek, Barry Bachman, and Todd Fahey on the boys' teams. And Isobel Rodriguez, Vanessa Haddix, and Luna Martin on the girls' teams. Stand up, kids."

Isobel stands up, feeling embarrassed but proud. Everyone is looking at her and clapping, but the only person she's thinking about is Roger. She sneaks a peek at him. He meets her eye and gives her the thumbs-up sign.

"Excuse me," Vanessa pipes up. "I'd like to make an announcement. I've really enjoyed being a part of Santa Barbara High's surf team, but soon I'll be making a change. My family is moving to Crescent Cove."

Isobel gasps. Vanessa is moving *here*? She glances at her friends, who look just as stunned as she feels.

"That's right," Vanessa goes on. "The big contests are here, the major surf companies are here, and soon I will be, too!"

"Well, welcome, Vanessa," Coach Daily says, looking a little stunned himself. Then he raises his trophy over his head and exclaims, "Okay, everybody, thanks for a great surf meet. Now, let's eat!"

But Isobel and her friends are too shocked to take a single bite. "I can't believe she's moving here," Luna exclaims.

"She's so full of herself," Rae grumbles. "Like we're supposed to stop in the middle of Coach Daily's toast to hear about her personal life?"

"I guess she thinks we're going to fall all over her with joy and gratitude," Kanani says.

Cricket groans. "Do you know what this means? Vanessa is going to be surfing at our spots, showing up at our hangouts, going to our school even."

"Come on, you guys," Isobel breaks in. "Don't you think you're being a little harsh? I mean, who knows? Vanessa might be really nice once you get to know her."

Everyone stares at her, but Isobel isn't about to back down. She doesn't believe in judging a person until she really knows her. No matter what anyone thinks, she's going to give Vanessa a chance.

"You're a good person, Isobel," Kanani says, touching her arm.

"Okay, we'll give her a chance," Cricket says grudgingly.

Silence falls over the table as everyone starts in on the food. Then out of the corner of her eye, Isobel notices Vanessa walk over to the karaoke machine at the corner of the patio. She puts in some money and the opening notes of Pink's "Get the Party Started" blasts through the speakers. Vanessa grabs the microphone and starts to sing.

Isobel can feel her mouth fall open. Vanessa can really sing! She knows how to move, too. Pretty soon, the whole patio is watching Vanessa and clapping along. The boys are whooping and hollering encouragement. Half a dozen kids get up and dance.

Isobel gulps. One of the boys who's jumped to his

feet is Roger. He's dancing with a girl from the surf clinic, but he's looking at Vanessa. In fact, he can't take his eyes off of her. He looks really interested, really impressed—in fact, he looks totally love-struck.

Get up and dance with him, Isobel tells herself. *Show him Vanessa isn't the only hot girl at this party.*

But she can't do it. She's just too intimidated.

Vanessa shakes her hips while she belts out the final chorus. Everyone gazes at her, spellbound. Isobel sinks down in her chair. She may have won the surf meet, but right now she feels like a total loser.

4

*I*sobel is certain she couldn't be more different from her brothers if she tried. While they play a game called Tank Wars on their PlayStation, she lies on the couch reading a collection of poetry.

"You're dead!" Miguel shouts triumphantly as he bombs Toni's tank.

"Oh, man!" Toni moans. "Just wait till the next game. I'm going to crush you!"

Isobel checks her watch. "Off," she orders.

"What?" the twins wail in disbelief.

"Mom said you have to stop playing at four o'clock and do your homework."

"Aaw!" they moan, but Isobel doesn't back down and eventually they shuffle off to their room.

Isobel returns to her book. Not many people know she loves to read poetry, and even fewer know she has tried writing some herself. One of the few who does know is Rae. She's sort of a poet herself; she plays the guitar and writes songs. Recently, she saw Isobel scribbling some lines in a notebook and begged to read them. Now Rae wants to put music to Isobel's words and turn them into a song.

Thinking of her poem, reciting it silently, Isobel can't help thinking of Roger.

Paddling hard, feeling a wall of water
Rise beneath me, I'm suddenly falling
Falling into the unknown,
Hoping I can hold on.
Half petrified, half exhilarated,
I'm wondering if I will tame this wave
Or be crushed under its foaming fist.

I think falling in love must be
A little like dropping in.
Someday I'll find that big wave
Of emotion and paddle into it.
Half petrified, half exhilarated,
I'll ride my heart into the unknown.

Isobel sighs. She remembers how she felt when Roger sat down next to her at the Beachside Grill. Her head was spinning, her stomach was somersaulting, her tongue was tied in knots. *Half petrified, half exhilarated.* Yep, that pretty much describes it.

Could this be love? she wonders.

But then she remembers the dreamy look in Roger's eyes when he watched Vanessa sing. Later, Isobel saw them talking together. And when the party ended and Isobel left with the surf team, Roger didn't even bother to come over to say good-bye.

If this is love, she thinks sadly, *it's pretty one-sided.*

Still, Isobel can't seem to put Roger out of her mind. For the fourth time in twenty-four hours, she goes to the computer and looks him up in the online phone directory. There are two Copenhavers listed in San Clemente—a Thomas Copenhaver and an R. C. Copenhaver. Could the second one be Roger?

She walks to the phone and picks it up. What will she say if he answers?

"Hi, Roger. How's the surf there?"

"Hey, Roger. Just wanted to ask you a few questions about getting sponsored."

"Roger, you hottie, do you realize I'm madly in love with you?"

Okay, that last one is out of the question, but the first two are perfectly reasonable conversation starters. Quickly, before she can change her mind, she dials the number. It rings twice and then she loses her nerve. Heart racing, she slams down the receiver.

"Hi, honey. Who were you talking to?"

Isobel looks up to find her mother walking in the door with a bag of groceries in her arms.

"Wrong number," she mumbles.

"Help me with this, will you?" Mami asks, handing

Isobel the bag as she takes off her jacket. "Abuelo and Abuelita are coming over for dinner tonight to celebrate your surf victory."

Isobel smiles. She loves her grandparents and their stories of growing up in Mexico. "What are we having for dinner?"

"Tri-tip."

"Yippee!" Miguel and Toni shout, appearing in the doorway.

"Did you do your homework?" Mami asks.

"Most of it," Miguel says.

"Well, finish it. Then come back and set the table. It's a warm night. I think we'll eat on the deck."

Isobel and Mami spend the next hour cooking pinto beans and rice and making fresh salsa and salad. When Papi gets home from work, he goes out to the deck to fire up the barbecue.

Abuelo and Abuelita arrive soon after that. "Where is my surfer girl?" Abuelo calls in his lilting accent.

Isobel hugs him. His white mustache tickles as he kisses her cheek.

"First place!" Abuelita exclaims. She's a short, stocky woman who comes up only to Isobel's shoulder. Her black hair is pulled back into a bun, and turquoise earrings dangle from her ears. "Did you get a trophy?"

"The team got a trophy," Isobel explains. "The top three boys and girls got medals."

"Put it on," Mami says. "Show your grandparents how it looks."

"Oh, Mami, I'd feel silly."

"In front of your family?" Abuelo protests. "No, no. You deserve to strut a little. Put it on, *mi nieta*."

Giggling, Isobel goes to her room and gets the medal. As she puts it over her head, her grandparents applaud.

"It's huge," Toni says disapprovingly.

"It looks like you're wearing a sewer cover on your chest," Miguel declares.

"Oh, you boys!" Abuelita scolds. "You're just jealous."

"I remember last summer when you two won skateboarding trophies," Abuelo points out. "You carried them with you everywhere and boasted to everyone how good you were. But Isobel never teased you, not once."

Listening to her family's friendly banter, Isobel feels a warm glow inside. When she's with them, she forgets to worry about her weight and her less-than-perfect looks. She stops caring about who likes her and who doesn't. With them, she feels smart, popular, and beautiful.

"The tri-tip is ready," Papi calls from the deck.

They all take their places around the picnic table. It's a beautiful late September evening. The cool, rainy weather hasn't arrived yet, so the air is still warm. Salad, rice, and beans are passed around. Papi slices the tri-tip. He serves Abuelo and Abuelita first, then passes the serving tray to the others.

"*Delicioso!*" Abuelo exclaims as he takes a bite.

"Eat up, Isobel," Abuelita says. "You need to stay strong so you can win more surf contests."

"My, my," Abuelo muses, taking a bite of his salad, "it is truly amazing what young girls can do these days. When I was growing up, girls were expected to stay home and help their mothers take care of the house."

"That was back when dinosaurs roamed the earth," Abuelita jokes. "Nowadays girls can snowboard, surf, climb mountains, even go into outer space."

"Now that I think about it," Abuelo says, glancing at his wife, "you weren't as sheltered as your parents might have thought." He looks around the table. "The first time I laid eyes on your grandmother, she was swimming in the ocean. I was walking on the beach, a boy from Mexico City, seeing the ocean for the first time. Suddenly, a vision appeared before me—a beautiful mermaid rose from the sea!"

"Really?" Toni gasps.

"It was Abuelita, stupid," Miguel chides him.

"But she was as lovely as a mermaid, and just as graceful in the water," Abuelo insists.

"My mother was afraid of the ocean," Abuelita says. "Her sister had drowned when she was only three. But I couldn't stay away. I used to pretend I was a dolphin who had been turned into a human by an evil sorcerer. I was sure that someday my dolphin prince would come break the spell. Then we would swim away together."

"Instead, all she got was me." Abuelo laughs.

"That was not such a bad thing," Abuelita says, touching his cheek.

"I guess I'm just like you, Mom," Mami says, smiling at Abuelita. She turns to Isobel. "I've always loved the water, too. But since we lived in Texas when I was growing up, far from the ocean, I had to make do with the local swimming pool."

"You did more than make do," Abuelita declares, turning to Isobel and her brothers. "You know your mother won many swimming medals when she was in high school. Yes, she was a dolphin, too."

Isobel smiles. She's heard about her mother's medals many times, but until last year, she had never seen them. Then, when they were packing up their belongings to move to California, Mami discovered them in a box in the attic.

"Don't pack them up again," Isobel had begged her. "You should keep them out. Maybe frame them."

"No, no," Mami had said with a laugh. "I'm proud of my accomplishments, but it's your turn to shine now."

As Papi sits back in his chair, he takes a sip of water. "Snowboarding, skateboarding, surfing—they're fun and they keep you healthy. But remember, kids, school is still number one. Without a good education, you won't get far in life."

Isobel picks at her rice. School is okay. She gets good grades, especially in English, History, and Spanish. But she has no idea what she wants to be when she grows up. Besides surfing, snowboarding, and poetry, there isn't anything that really interests her.

Isobel thinks about Rae's old boyfriend, Shane Fox. He dropped out of school to become a professional surfer. Okay, he isn't exactly rich, but he gets to travel around the world and surf every day. Plus, he has lots of fans, he gets all his boards for free, and he sure seems to be having fun.

Isobel can't help thinking Shane's life sounds pretty wonderful. But her parents and grandparents would freak if she told them she didn't want to go to college.

Abuelo's voice brings her back to the moment. "Thank you for another wonderful dinner," he says, putting down his fork.

"You're always welcome," Mami replies. She and Abuelita start to clear the table. Isobel, Miguel, and Toni help. Papi and Abuelo sit at the edge of the patio, smoking cigars and talking.

"Abuelita," Toni says, "come to my room and see my spelling test. I got every word right."

"Big deal," Miguel scoffs. "I got an A+ on my California topographical map."

"I want to see them both," Abuelita says. "But a little bird told me that Isobel's picture was in the newspaper. First, I want to see that."

Eagerly, Isobel leads Abuelita to her room. The photo is on her bulletin board. It shows her roaring across the face of a six-foot wave during the finals.

"Look at you!" Abuelita exclaims. "You're going so fast! Weren't you scared?"

"Maybe a little," Isobel admits. "But I was excited, too." She sits on her bed. "There was a surfer there, a boy who was helping out at the surf clinic. He said I could be a really good big-wave surfer someday if I keep at it. He even said I was good enough to be sponsored."

Abuelita looks at Isobel thoughtfully. "Who is this boy? Did he tell you his name?"

"Sure. It's Roger. Why?"

"I saw a light turn on in your eyes when you mentioned him. It might have been his words that moved you, but I think maybe it was him. Am I right?"

"Oh, Abuelita," Isobel laughs, waving her hand dismissively.

"Now, now, come on. I know how it is with young girls. Do you think I wasn't young once? You heard the story of your grandfather watching me on the beach. Do you suppose I wasn't looking at him, too?"

Isobel giggles. "Well, okay, you're right. I do like Roger. And at first I thought he liked me, too. But then later, at the party, he was looking at another girl—a surfer who's everything I'm not."

"What do you mean?" Abuelita asks.

"She's gorgeous, and she knows it. She got up in front of everybody and sang. I'd rather die than do something like that."

"This girl may be a diamond, but you are a pearl, Isobel," Abuelita says with conviction.

"But how do I know if Roger likes pearls?"

Abuelita chuckles. Then she slips her arm around Isobel's waist. "After I met your grandfather on the beach, he returned to Mexico City. Would I ever see him again? I wondered. I confided my feelings to my grandmother. I will tell you what she told me. 'Be patient, *mi nieta*. If it's meant to be, you will meet again.'"

Isobel smiles. She knows the end of the story. Abuelo and Abuelita wrote letters to each other for two long years. Then one day, Abuelo came back for her. They've been together ever since.

Will Roger and I love each other like that? Isobel wonders. She hopes so. She just prays it won't be two years before she sees him again!

5

*T*wo weeks later, Isobel is standing in front of the high school, talking with her friends, when a shiny yellow Subaru Baja cruises into the parking lot.

"Sweet truck," Luna remarks.

Apparently other people think so, too. Heads turn as the truck pulls into a parking space. Then the door opens and out steps Vanessa Haddix.

"Oh, no," Rae moans.

"I was hoping her parents would change their minds about moving here," Cricket says.

"Look at her," Kanani mutters as Vanessa struts toward the school. "She's knows everyone's checking her out."

"You can bet the boys are," Isobel remarks.

Sure enough, Vanessa is barely out of the parking lot before the guys from the surf team surround her.

Luna laughs. " 'Look at me!' " she preens, imitating Vanessa, " 'I'm so special!' "

The girls snicker, all except Isobel, who remarks, "I think we're just jealous of her."

"Hardly!" Rae explodes.

"I might be if she wasn't so totally full of herself," Kanani says. "Look at her. It makes me want to gag."

Isobel looks. Vanessa is flipping her silky blonde hair over her shoulder and giggling as the surf team boys fall all over themselves to get close to her. The expression on their faces is just like the one Roger wore when Vanessa was singing—dreamy and drooling.

Isobel sighs. Yes, Vanessa is over the top. But apparently, that's what boys want.

The girls are giggling among themselves, but Isobel isn't listening. She tries to imagine herself flirting and teasing the way Vanessa does, but it's impossible. For one thing, she's way too shy and self-conscious even to attempt something like that. For another, she doesn't have Vanessa's perfect figure, her high cheekbones, or her pouty lips—not to mention her pierced belly button!

"Why bother flirting if you don't have anything to show off?" Isobel wonders.

"What?" Kanani asks.

Isobel shrugs with embarrassment. She hadn't meant to say that out loud.

"Don't look now, but I think her royal highness is about to acknowledge our presence," Rae whispers.

Sure enough, Vanessa is walking toward them. "Hey!" she calls. "Here I am, as promised."

"Hi," all the girls reply. Rae looks as if she's about to say something else, but she stops herself.

"This school is smaller than my old school," Vanessa announces. "Plainer, too. Santa Barbara High looks like an old Spanish fort. What's your swimming pool like?"

"It's got all the important stuff," Luna replies dryly. "A diving board, lane lines, water."

Vanessa laughs. "Good. I'll probably join the swim team. Water polo, too. We have surf team practice this afternoon, right?"

Kanani nods. "Three-thirty at Luna Bay."

Vanessa looks at Luna. "Luna's your name, isn't it?"

"The break is named after her," Rae pipes up. "She's been surfing there since she was three."

"Impressive," Vanessa remarks. "All I've got is a bathing suit named after me."

"What?" Rae asks with a frown.

Vanessa smiles smugly. "Eels is putting out a Vanessa Haddix signature bikini. I'll be wearing it this afternoon."

Isobel can't believe it. Eels brand bikinis are in all the local surf shops. And now Vanessa has one named after her. *No wonder she's strutting around like she's something special*, Isobel thinks.

"Well, the boys offered to walk me to my home-room," Vanessa says. "Guess I'd better get going."

"Sounds like a good idea," Cricket says disdainfully.

If Vanessa gets Cricket's meaning, she doesn't let

on. "I think I'm going to like it here," she says thoughtfully. Then she wiggles her fingers and says, "Later," as she walks away to meet the boys.

"Here she comes," Luna announces as Vanessa drives her Baja into the parking lot of Crescent Cove Beach Park.

The girls look up from waxing their boards. "She's ten minutes late," Kanani says, checking her watch.

"She was late to History, too," Kanani adds. "She told the teacher she couldn't find the room." She shakes her head. "With the entire boys' surf team leading her around? I don't *think* so!"

"You should have seen her in homeroom," Rae says. "She talked nonstop to Barry Bachman the whole time Mr. Collingswood was calling the roll. Then, when he was finished, she raised her hand and asked, 'Did you call Vanessa Haddix?' When Mr. Collingswood said yes, Vanessa shot him this annoying little smile and said, 'Here.' "

"Are you serious?" Luna cries. "That is so rude!"

Vanessa bounces out of the truck and grabs her board. Like robots, the boys leap to their feet and hurry to meet her.

"That must be the bikini she was telling us about," Rae says, checking out Vanessa's athletic-cut black-and-pink-striped bathing suit.

"Pretty hot," Isobel comments.

No one can deny it.

"So how about this famous Luna Bay," Vanessa says, walking up to join them. She surveys the three-foot waves peeling off Black Rock. "I hope it gets bigger than this once in a while."

"Oh, it does," Luna answers. "It closes out at about eight feet. Four to six feet is perfect. You can ride the rights all the way to the shore. The lefts are a little smaller, but still sweet."

"Vanessa, welcome!" the coach breaks in. "I'm Coach Daily."

As predicted, Vanessa smiles sweetly and replies, "Sorry I'm late. I got lost."

"It's not easy finding your way around a new town," he agrees. "Now let's see how you do surfing a new break."

"Piece of cake," she answers.

While Vanessa puts on her wet suit and waxes her board, the rest of the team paddles out. Coach Daily joins them on his longboard. "Let's wait for her," he says.

Clearly, the boys don't mind. They're happy to sit in the water, watching Vanessa get ready. But the girls huddle together, frustrated that they have to let a perfect set go by.

"Did you see her at lunch?" Cricket asks, chomping on a fat wad of bubblegum. "She was bragging to everybody about all the famous surfers she knows."

"Like who?" Isobel asks.

"Like Shane Fox."

The girls crack up. Rae dated Shane over the summer and eventually dropped him because he was so self-centered and egotistical. "I'm not surprised they're friends," she mutters. "They're two of a kind."

Finally, Vanessa is ready. She paddles out and, without so much as a glance toward the team, immediately takes off on a wave.

"We waited for her," Luna cries, turning to Coach Daily. "Why didn't she wait for us?"

"I think she's just excited," the coach responds. "This is a new break for her. She wants to try it out."

But Isobel suspects Vanessa just wants to show everyone how good she is. And it's true. She's totally ripping, pulling off manic cutbacks that throw up huge fans of whitewater. She ends her ride with a picture-perfect off-the-lip that makes the coach let out a long, low whistle.

"She's so good, it's scary!" Dwayne Potter exclaims.

"We're going to win every meet this season," Maddie Pillsbury predicts. "No doubt about it."

"We could win every meet even without her," Cricket retorts, grinding her bubblegum hard. "We've won the first three, haven't we? And we were competing *against* Vanessa in the first meet."

"Okay, kids, we're a team, remember?" Coach Daily says, glancing with disapproval at Cricket. "Having Vanessa join us can only make us stronger. So let's work together, okay?"

Cricket scowls and takes off on the next wave,

47

shredding it at hyper-speed. *She looks good,* Isobel thinks, *but she doesn't have Vanessa's fluid moves.*

"Nice ride, Vanessa," Coach says when she returns to the lineup.

"Thanks. That girl who just took off really likes to rip, doesn't she?"

Coach chuckles. "Cricket lives up to her name, that's for sure."

Vanessa frowns. "She's not responding to what the wave is doing. She needs to slow down and get focused."

"Good point," Coach Daily replies. "I'll talk to her about that."

Kanani looks at Isobel and rolls her eyes. "Vanessa thinks she knows more than the coach does," she whispers disdainfully.

"She's kind of right though," Isobel points out.

"Well, yeah, but so what? It's Coach Daily's job to critique us, not hers. And what's with him—sucking up to her like she's Layne Beachley! Puh-leeze!"

Isobel laughs. Vanessa is amazing, but she isn't a four-time world champion—not yet, anyway. Besides, Kanani is right. Vanessa shouldn't be critiquing the other surfers on her team. That's the coach's job.

The rest of the afternoon passes quickly as the team members practice their moves on wave after wave. Later, on the shore, everyone dries off, and the coach hands out Gatorade and Balance Bars.

"I've only been in town a few days, and I'm getting bored already," Vanessa says when the coach is out of earshot. She stretches out her legs and flips her damp hair over her shoulders. "What do you guys do around here for excitement?"

"Rae's mom owns horses and leads guided rides," Isobel says. "You can go on a trail ride or a beach ride. It's pretty cool."

"There's the mall," Barry adds.

"And the skateboard park," says Dwayne.

"Guys, I'm talking excitement," Vanessa replies, wrinkling her perfect nose. "You know, something extreme."

"My older brother went night-surfing at the pier once," Jed suggests. "That might be kind of cool."

"Or kind of stupid," Kanani says. "It's hard enough to avoid hitting the pilings when you can see them. At night, who knows what might happen?"

"Oh, come on, don't be such a wimp," Vanessa says. "We're not beginners. We can take care of ourselves."

"I'm not a wimp," Kanani protests.

"Then let's do it. I dare you."

"I'm in," Barry says. "But we have to wait until the next full moon."

"I'll be there," Vanessa declares.

"Me, too," Dwayne and Jed say together.

No one speaks for a moment. Then Rae pipes up, "I'll go."

"All right!" Vanessa laughs. "At least one of you girls isn't chicken."

"None of us are chicken," Rae shoots back. "We'll all be there, won't we, girls?"

Isobel swallows hard. She's never been night-surfing

before, and she's not sure she wants to, especially since she knows it will mean lying to her parents to get out of the house. Still, she isn't about to let her girlfriends down. And really, Vanessa is so full of herself! Isobel is dying to show her that anything she can do, the surfer girls of Crescent Cove can do better.

"The night of the next full moon, south side of the pier," Isobel says firmly. "Be there."

The girls slap high fives. Vanessa finishes her Balance Bar and tosses the wrapper onto her towel. "You can count on it," she says with a smile.

6

Who knew working in a surf shop could be so boring?" Cricket moans as Luna rips open yet another carton filled with boxes of surfboard leashes.

"And you thought it was all glamour and glitz," Luna laughs. "No, my friends." She assumes the voice of a hardened TV newswoman. "Tonight on *20/20*— the painful reality of surf-shop life revealed."

Rae grabs a tube of sunscreen that's lying on a nearby shelf and holds it to her mouth like a microphone. "Tell me, Cricket, what's it like working at Shoreline Surf Shop?"

"We're nothing but slave labor," Cricket wails into Rae's sunscreen microphone. "All we do is open boxes and slap price tags on surf gear. Hour after hour without a break. It's inhuman!"

"It's all her fault," Rae says, tossing aside the sunscreen and pointing at Kanani. "If she hadn't talked me into sneaking out of our motel room to look for that loser—"

"Oh, please!" Kanani laughs. "You didn't think he was a loser when we were in Florida. 'J.T.,'" she squeals, mimicking Rae, "'I love you! I love you!'"

Isobel snickers. She's heard this story a dozen times since Luna, Rae, and Kanani returned from a recent longboarding contest in Florida, but it always fascinates her. While they were there, Kanani and Rae both fell for the same boy and almost destroyed their friendship fighting over him. Then, when a dangerous hurricane hit the coast, they joined forces and sneaked out of their motel room to search for him.

Isobel can't imagine risking her friendship with one of the girls for anything—not even a boy. Luna, Rae, Kanani, and Cricket are like her second family. When she moved to Crescent Cove and didn't know a soul, it was Kanani who befriended her and taught her how to surf. Later, when they met Luna, Rae, and Cricket out in the water, the five of them clicked immediately. They've been as tight as a fist ever since.

"Hey, just be grateful we all agreed to share your jail sentence," Cricket says.

As punishment for sneaking off without asking permission, Luna's parents sentenced Kanani and Rae to work fifty hours without pay in their surf shop. Isobel, Luna, and Cricket agreed to work, too, just to give their friends moral support.

"If that isn't friendship, I don't know what is," Isobel proclaims, although they all know that working at Shoreline Surf is more fun than drudgery.

Except now. If Isobel has to unpack, price, and shelve one more carton of surfboard leashes, fins, or surf wax, she's sure she's going to scream.

"Okay," Luna says, glancing through the inventory sheets that her parents have given her. "Women's tall UGG boots, $115 a pair. Ready, set, start pricing!"

As the girls raise their sticker guns, Tuck sticks his head into the back room. "Isobel," he says, "there's someone here looking for you."

"Me?" She can't imagine anyone who would be looking for her, except maybe her brothers. But Miguel and Toni are over at the Boys and Girls Club, playing roller hockey.

A sudden chill runs down her spine. Did something happen? Is one of them hurt or in trouble?

Tossing down her sticker gun, she rushes into the store, only to find Roger standing there with a big grin on his face.

"Roger!" she gasps as her heart leaps into overdrive. "W-what are you doing here?"

"Looking for you," he replies. "Can you take a break?"

Isobel looks around for Tuck and is surprised to find him standing right behind her. "Sure," he says before she can utter a word. "You're scheduled to work another hour, but you can blow it off. I won't tell the boss if you don't."

Isobel laughs—Tuck *is* the boss. She takes a step toward Roger, wondering which emotion she's feeling more—joy or horror. She's thrilled to see Roger again, no doubt about that. But what will she say to him? How should she act? Her mouth feels dry, her feet are leaden, and her brain is a total blank.

Somehow, she manages to remember to grab her backpack from the back room. The girls, who have been spying through a crack in the door, burst into shrieks of delight.

She hushes them, blushing furiously. "He'll hear!" she hisses.

"He likes you, Isobel," Cricket exclaims. "Big time."

"So where are you going with him?" Kanani asks.

"I-I don't know." Isobel gulps.

"Take him for a walk on the beach," Luna suggests.

"Then trip on a rock and fall into his arms," Rae adds with a giggle.

Isobel grimaces at the thought, but the girls just laugh. Kanani grabs her and fluffs up her hair while Luna brushes a wrinkle from her T-shirt. Rae hands her a tube of lip gloss. Isobel brushes it aside, feeling more nervous than ever.

"Good luck," she hears her friends whisper as she stumbles out of the back room.

But where is Roger? Did he get impatient and leave? Isobel feels simultaneously crushed and relieved until Tuck points toward the sidewalk. Roger is standing outside, waiting for her.

As Isobel walks out the door, he turns and unleashes a dazzling smile. "Surprised to see me?"

"Totally," she answers honestly.

"So you didn't get my phone message."

"What message?"

"I called you about a week ago. I left a message with your father."

Oh, my gosh! she thinks. *He called me! He called me!*

But then she realizes she has to explain about her embarrassing, infuriating father. "Papi can get a little weird sometimes," she begins. "If a boy calls, he just conveniently forgets to tell me."

"But what if it's someone from school calling for a homework assignment or something?" Roger asks.

"I know; it's crazy. I don't think he's ready to face the fact I'm not a little kid anymore. Mami, either."

"Wait a minute. How old are you?"

"Sixteen," she whispers, certain he'll decide she's much too young for him.

But instead he says, "Your parents better wake up. If they want to keep boys away from you, they're going to have to lock you in a tower and hire a dragon."

Isobel is speechless. Does Roger actually think boys are clamoring to spend time with her? As if! Of course, Roger is a boy, and he actually went to the trouble of tracking her down. Still, she can't quite believe he likes her. There must be some other reason why he's here.

"So how did you find me?" she asks.

"Well, at first I figured you didn't call because you weren't interested," he says. "But I couldn't stop thinking about you, and finally I decided to give it one more try. This time I got your brother on the phone. He told me you'd be working at Shoreline Surf after school. So here I am."

The words *I couldn't stop thinking about you* are echoing in Isobel's head. *Wow,* she thinks, *maybe he does like me!*

"So," she says stupidly, "here you are."

"Yeah." He laughs, looking almost as self-conscious as she feels. "So, uh, you want to go for a walk or something?"

"Okay," she says, remembering Luna's advice. "The beach is only a couple of blocks away."

"Let's go."

They head down Surf Street, past Mort's Bait Shop and the Surf-N-Taco. It's all so familiar to Isobel, yet suddenly different and special with Roger by her side. At Crescent Cove Beach Park, they take off their shoes and step onto the sand.

"Nice little waves," Roger remarks, gazing out at the ocean.

"That's Luna Bay," she says. "It was named after my friend."

She tells Roger the story—how Luna learned to surf here, how her father started calling it Luna Bay, and how the name caught on among local surfers. "Now, when you look in a surfing guide," Isobel explains, "you'll find Luna Bay listed as the official name."

"Cool," Roger says. "Maybe someday there'll be a surf spot named after you."

"Oh, sure. Wipeout Point."

He laughs. "Which way should we go?"

"Let's head north. It's not as crowded, and sometimes you can see sea lions on the rocks."

They start walking, and Roger asks, "Have you been in any big surf since the contest?"

She shakes her head. "It's been pretty flat around here lately."

"That's why you've got to travel. It's like I told you. You gotta go where the waves are."

"Yeah, but it's like *I* told *you*," she counters. "I have school during the week, and I work at my dad's store on weekends. Besides, my parents would never let me take off on a surf safari. I'm lucky if I can convince them to let me go downtown on a Saturday night."

"I keep forgetting you're in high school," he says with a sigh. "You seem older. And you definitely surf older."

"Thanks," she answers, beaming and blushing at the same time. "What about you? Are you a big-wave junkie, too?"

"Definitely. I go down to Baja three or four times a year. You would love it—miles and miles of empty beaches, surf of every shape and size. Then there's the jewel of Baja Sur—Todos Santos."

Isobel has read about Todos Santos. It's a killer big-wave spot, one of the best in the world. "You've surfed Todos?" she asks with awe.

"Twice. It was mind-boggling. First time I broke my board and almost broke my neck. Second time I did much better. I'm going back this winter."

Isobel feels a shiver slide down her spine at the thought of riding a wave like that. And yet, it excites her, too. Maybe someday she'll have the skill and courage it takes to try it.

"You'll go there someday," he says as if he's reading her mind.

She shrugs. Right now it's hard to imagine ever leaving home. Her family is like a rock, always there for her to hold on to. But sometimes they feel more like a weight she'd like to throw off.

"What's it like to be in college?" she asks.

"It's more work than high school. More responsibility, too. But I like being on my own, making my own plans, dealing with the consequences if I screw up."

"What are you majoring in?"

"Business," he replies. "I'd like to work for a surf company someday."

"You don't want to be a professional surfer?" she asks.

"I don't think I'm good enough. Or maybe I just don't want it bad enough. But I do want to spend my life surfing. That's why I think working for a surf company would be the perfect job for me."

"Oh, look!" Isobel cries. "Sea lions!"

A large, flat rock juts up out of the water about twenty yards offshore. Five fat sea lions are sprawled across it, basking in the sun. Two younger ones swim around the rock, looking for a spot to jump on. But each time one tries, the larger sea lions honk and snap at it.

"They're just like people," Roger says. "They could share that rock or take turns, but they'd rather fight over it."

"Why are we like that?" Isobel wonders.

"I don't know," he replies. "All I know is I don't like it. That's why sometimes I wonder why I'm majoring in Business. I'm just not into all that cutthroat wheeling and dealing."

"That's not a bad thing," she replies. "I mean, the world could use more businessmen who believe in ethics and honesty."

"You think so?" Roger says.

She nods and looks up at him. There's something so right about the way she feels standing next to him. Part of it, she decides, is his physical presence. He's only a couple of inches taller than she is, with a strength and solidity that mirrors her own. When she's with him, she doesn't feel too heavy, too muscular, too anything. She feels just right.

Then their eyes lock, and she feels her brain start to melt. There's electricity in the air, and it occurs to her that he might kiss her.

The thought scares her. Quickly, she backs away and looks at her watch. "I'd better get back. I told my parents I'd be home by five."

"Five? That's over an hour from now."

"It . . . it is?" she stammers foolishly. "Well, still—"

"*Tengo hambre,*" he says suddenly. "*¿Quieres algo para comer?*"

"*Sí,*" she answers, slipping easily into Spanish. "*¿Por qué no?*"

"How about that Surf-N-Taco place? *¿Es bueno?*"

She nods. "The shrimp tacos are killer."

"Seriously? I love shrimp tacos. Not every place has them."

"Then get ready to get happy."

He laughs and reaches for her hand. She tenses, and he turns to her, a worried expression on his face. "I'm sorry. I just thought—"

"I . . . no . . . it's just . . ." *Just what?* she wonders. Her head is spinning, and her knees feel shaky. No one has ever made her feel like this before, and it scares her. But she likes it, too. She likes it a lot.

There's an awkward pause as he stands there, still holding her hand. Then he gives it a gentle squeeze and lets it fall. "There'll be plenty of time for holding hands later," he says, "after we get to know each other better. And, Isobel, I do want to get to know you better."

She's so stunned, she can barely speak. "Me, too," she manages to utter.

He grins. "Race you back to Surf Street!" he shouts, and takes off running.

For a moment she just stands there, too surprised to move. Then she laughs and starts after him, running as fast as she can.

7

I'll never forget it," Luna says as she drives along the waterfront. "There was Rae, just screaming down the line. And then I realize, oh, no, she's going to shoot the pier. I'm not kidding, my heart was in my throat."

"I almost pulled it off, too," Rae proclaims from the backseat. "But the wave closed out, and I was forced to cut toward shore. Suddenly, I saw this big, honkin' piling coming at me. I just closed my eyes and bailed."

Isobel gazes out the passenger-side window. In the light of the full moon, the Crescent Cove Pier looks hulking and ghostly. She tries to imagine surfing between its pilings. Just the thought of it makes her stomach lurch.

"Then I saw her hit a piling, and I thought it was all over," Luna continues. "But she popped up and swam out with nothing but a few bruises."

"I'm going to try it again someday," Rae promises. "I'm going to make it, too."

"How about tonight?" Cricket suggests with a giggle.

"No way!" Kanani breaks in. "I don't want anyone trying anything stupid. We're just going to surf a few waves and go home, okay?"

"Okay, Mom," Luna says sarcastically.

"I'm serious," Kanani insists. "This whole thing is stupid. We don't have to prove anything to Vanessa."

"You can say that again," Cricket mutters.

Isobel nibbles on the corner of her fingernail. Kanani's words make her wonder what they're doing here. Not that there's any reason to be afraid, she tells herself. The moon is so bright, she could read a book by it.

Luna parks the Jeep at the curb and the girls pile out. They take their surfboards from the roof and jog across the sand to the water's edge. The surf team boys are already there—Jed, Barry, Dwayne, Terrell, and Kristian, along with Maddie Pillsbury, who has recently started going out with Dwayne.

"You seen Vanessa?" Dwayne asks around a mouthful of Chee•tos.

"Can I have some of those?" Cricket asks, reaching for the bag. She can never resist junk food. But to Isobel, whose stomach is filled with butterflies, they look disgusting.

"Maybe she chickened out," Rae suggests.

"Not a chance," Vanessa says, stepping out of the darkness. The boys draw closer, like moths to a flame.

"Everybody ready?" Jed asks. The whole crew nods.

"Stick together, and let's keep an eye on each other," Kanani warns.

"What do you think we're going to find out there?" Vanessa laughs. "The Loch Ness monster?"

She splashes into the water and throws her board down. The boys follow eagerly, and the girls bring up the rear. The water feels cold on Isobel's feet, and she wishes she had brought her booties. But it's too late for that now. She hops on her board and starts to paddle.

The waves breaking against the pier sound unnaturally loud in the stillness. Moonlight shimmers on the water, making the whitewater look silver. But the pilings cast long, dark shadows, and each time Isobel paddles through one, she feels a scary shiver slip down her spine.

Luna paddles up beside her and smiles. Isobel tries to smile back, but the corner of her mouth keeps twitching involuntarily. "This is giving me the creeps," she admits.

"It's the same water we surf in during the daytime," Luna reminds her. "Just a little darker, that's all."

But that's the problem. Isobel has always been afraid of the dark. It reminds her of boogeymen with bloodshot eyes and maniacs in hockey masks. She's never told her friends, but she used a night-light until she was twelve, and even now, she often leaves the closet light on.

Soon, everyone reaches the lineup. It's hard to judge the waves in the moonlight. They seem to rear up out of nowhere, then quickly disappear.

"I was out here this morning," Barry says. "It was about shoulder-high."

"This is a pretty fast wave," Jed tells Vanessa. "Don't hesitate or you won't make it."

"I never hesitate," she says with a sly grin. "Haven't you figured that out yet?"

The boys laugh like Vanessa just said something unbelievably witty. Luna catches Isobel's eye with a look that says, *Give me a break!*

Suddenly, a black shape rears out of the water, just inches from Isobel's board. She gasps and jumps back, images of boogeymen and psycho killers in her head. Instantly, she loses her balance and falls off the board, arms flailing. Now she's thinking Loch Ness monster. She shrieks and practically levitates back onto her board.

It's only then that she realizes everyone is laughing at her. "Do you know what that was?" Vanessa snickers.

Isobel is gulping down air, too freaked to answer.

"A harbor seal," Luna answers with a giggle.

Jed raises his arms and wiggles his fingers threateningly. "A bloodthirsty killer harbor seal, in search of young surfer chicks to eat!"

The crew laughs even harder. Isobel looks away. Her face burns with embarrassment. Harbor seals never hurt people. They're totally benign. But how was she supposed to know it was a seal? All she could tell was that it was big, black, and coming at her.

The girls have stopped giggling, but the boys are still

hysterical. Dwayne is laughing so hard, he's snorting. Isobel knows she should take it in stride, just laugh along with them, but she's starting to get annoyed.

After all, it wasn't *that* funny. And in the darkness, that harbor seal really was scary. It's not as if she's a wimp or anything. Not by a long shot.

A wave rises behind her, big and tubey, and she decides to prove her point. She paddles—once, twice—and instantly, she's up and riding, ducking her head as the lip pitches out over her.

In the shadowy moonlight, she can hardly tell where she's going. Trying to ignore the nagging fear in the back of her brain, she keeps her eyes focused on the wave. Then suddenly, she sees the pier pilings looming in front of her. With a gasp, she kicks out.

The next thing she sees is someone surfing toward her. It's a girl, she can tell that much. Then the silhouette surfs closer, and she realizes it's Vanessa. Like Isobel, she kicks out as she approaches the pilings.

"Hey!" Vanessa calls as she begins paddling out. "Nice wave!"

"You, too."

Vanessa paddles over until they're floating side by side. "Sorry about the harbor seal. I probably would have wet myself if it happened to me."

Isobel laughs. "I almost did."

"And hey, I've been meaning to tell you, congratulations on winning the final heat against me in the surf meet. You were on fire."

Isobel feels her chest swell with pride. "Thanks. I got some good waves. But you surfed well, too. You always do."

Vanessa shrugs modestly. "You know, people think I'm so together, but it hasn't been easy moving to a new town and trying to fit in. The girls are all jealous of me, and the boys act like I'm some kind of surf goddess. It probably sounds more fun than it really is."

Isobel doesn't know what to make of Vanessa. She sounds like she's boasting, but her assessment isn't far off. The boys do treat her like a goddess. As for the girls being envious, Isobel can't speak for her friends, but jealousy is definitely an emotion she feels when she's around Vanessa. How can she help it? Vanessa has everything Isobel longs for—a gorgeous face, a perfect body, a happening surf career, and more brazen self-confidence than a rock star.

"Anyway," Vanessa says, "what I'm trying to say is, I could really use a friend. Someone like you."

"Me?" Isobel croaks in astonishment.

"Okay, never mind. I didn't mean to offend you. I just thought—"

"I'm not offended," Isobel answers quickly. The fact is she's flattered.

"You just seemed like the type of person I could be friends with," Vanessa continues. "You're really genuine and down-to-earth, you know?"

No one has ever given Isobel a compliment quite

like that before. It feels good. "Thanks," she says with a shy smile.

"So listen, I'm stoked to check out that surf spot north of town—Paintball Point. I'd love to have a local with me who can show me around. Do you want to come?"

"Sure. When?"

"I was thinking Saturday morning. Are you busy?"

"I have to work at my dad's store at ten," Isobel replies. "Let's go early, okay?"

"Definitely. I can meet you in the parking lot at seven. Will that work?"

Isobel nods. Looking up, she notices they're floating dangerously close to the pilings. "We'd better paddle out."

The girls dig in and soon join the lineup. "Where were you?" Kanani asks. "I was about ready to come looking for you."

"I was talking to Vanessa."

"Lucky you."

"She's not so bad."

Isobel pauses, wondering if she should tell Kanani and the other girls about the Saturday surf session at Paintball Point. But then she thinks better of it. The girls would probably want to come. Vanessa would be surprised and probably a little intimidated. Pretty soon the session would turn into some kind of challenge with everyone trying to outsurf one another.

No, better she should keep quiet. If she can spend

some time with Vanessa and really get to know her, maybe she can convince the girls they should get to know her, too. Then, eventually, they can all be friends.

Isobel smiles, relishing her new role as diplomat. She pictures a time in the future when Vanessa and the girls are all part of the same surf posse. "It never would have happened without you, Isobel," she imagines their saying.

Isobel feels so hopeful, she forgets to be afraid of the dark. She catches a couple more waves, banters with her friends, and cheers on the boys.

"Night-surfing is kind of cool," she tells Kanani.

Her friend is about to reply when suddenly they hear Jed exclaim, "There's no way you can pull that off!"

"You wanna bet?" Vanessa replies.

"Go on, then, show us," Barry says.

"What are they talking about?" Isobel asks Kanani.

Her friend shrugs. "I have no idea."

"Do you dare me?" Vanessa asks coyly.

"I double-dog dare you," Jed shoots back.

Vanessa grins. "Okay, boys, let me show you how it's done."

She lines up to wait for a wave. The boys gather around. Someone shouts, "Go for it, girl! Shoot the pier!"

Isobel and Kanani stare at each other, unable to believe what they've just heard. Vanessa is going to try and shoot the pier? At night?

Now all the boys are whooping and chanting, "Shoot the pier! Shoot the pier!"

Isobel looks around for her girlfriends. Luna and Cricket are nowhere in sight, but Rae is paddling toward Vanessa, calling, "Don't do it. It's too dangerous!"

But the words are barely out of her mouth when Vanessa takes off on a fast, pitching wave. She roars down the line and disappears into the tube.

Let it close out, Isobel prays. But it doesn't, and a moment later, she sees Vanessa's head pop up as she flies out the other side.

The pier is just ahead. "Bail out!" Isobel cries. "Bail out!"

A second later, Vanessa disappears into the shadows. Isobel holds her breath, waiting for the sound of impact as Vanessa slams into a piling.

But it doesn't happen, and, after a seemingly endless moment, Vanessa's voice can be heard, whooping triumphantly from the other side of the pier.

"She made it!" Jed cries with awe in his voice.

"That girl rules!" Dwayne shouts, ignoring the dirty look his girlfriend, Maddie, is giving him.

Now the boys are chanting, "Vanessa! Vanessa! Vanessa!"

She appears, grinning as she paddles out to join them.

"Told you I could do it," she says.

Terrell bows before her. "We are not worthy," he jokes.

The other boys join in, laughing and bowing. "We are not worthy!" they chant.

"So what else is new?" Vanessa chuckles. She looks around at the girls. "Anyone else want to try it?" she asks.

"No, thanks," Kanani says. "I'm not crazy enough to do anything that stupid."

"Yeah," Maddie agrees. "I like my face just the way it is. I don't need to have it rearranged by a piling."

"Besides," Rae mutters, "we don't have to prove anything to you."

Isobel doesn't say anything at all.

Vanessa shrugs. "Whatever. I'm heading in." She catches a wave and the boys follow her like lemmings.

Isobel paddles in, too, trying to make sense of what she's just witnessed. Shooting the pier at night was a really lamebrained thing to do. But instead of admiring the rest of the girls for refusing to attempt something so dangerous and stupid, the boys are acting like Vanessa just pulled off the coolest stunt they've ever seen.

Vanessa, Isobel decides, is really hard to figure out. One minute she's telling Isobel she could really use a friend, and the next she's doing everything in her power to one-up the rest of the girls.

Isobel sighs as she picks up her surfboard and walks to shore. Maybe playing diplomat is going to be harder than she thought.

8

*I*sobel is leaning on the hood of her car, waiting for Vanessa. The parking lot at Paintball Point is getting more crowded by the minute. Isobel checks her watch. Seven-twenty. "Hurry up, Vanessa," she whispers.

But part of her is hoping Vanessa doesn't show. Since their moonlight surf session, Isobel's been even more confused about Vanessa than she was before. Does Vanessa truly want to be friends with Isobel and her crew? Or is she just trying to show them up? Isobel can't figure it out.

She hears her cell phone ringing and opens the glove compartment to get it. Checking the caller I.D., she sees it's Kanani and decides to let voice mail answer. The girls wanted her to surf Luna Bay with them this morning, but she told them she had to clean her room. A white lie, but it doesn't feel good. Still, she doubts they would have understood why she's standing them up to surf with Vanessa.

Why am I? Isobel asks herself. And then she answers, trying to convince herself she knows what she's talking about. *Because I'm trying to build a bridge between Vanessa and the crew. Because we're all going to be friends someday.*

Just then, Vanessa drives her yellow Baja into the lot. She squeals to a halt next to Isobel's car and jumps out. "Sorry I'm late. I couldn't find my car keys."

"You have to put your keys in the same place every night," Isobel replies. "I learned that the hard way when I left them in my jeans and my mother washed them. It destroyed the remote door opener."

"That doesn't work in my house. I've got a younger brother and sister whose main goal in life is to mess up my stuff."

"I've got two ten-year-old brothers," Isobel says. "Twins."

"Twins?" Vanessa gasps. "My brother and sister are twins, too!"

"You poor thing," Isobel says with a laugh.

Vanessa rolls her eyes. "Tell me about it. They're twelve, and they think their God's gift to the universe. Everyone thinks they're *so* cute, but I know the truth. They're messengers from Satan!"

Isobel cracks up. Only someone with twins in the family—younger ones, especially—can know how it feels. And Vanessa obviously does. Suddenly, Isobel feels much closer to her than before.

The girls wax their boards and wriggle into the wet

suits, all the while exchanging stories about their annoying younger siblings. By the time they head down the trail that leads to the beach, they're laughing like old friends.

"This reminds me of Rincon," Vanessa remarks. "The trail to the beach there is lined with eucalyptus trees, too. Have you ever surfed there?"

"I wish! I've never surfed anywhere except Crescent Cove."

"Rincon is pretty much the perfect wave. It's crowded, but once your prove yourself, you've always got a place in the lineup." She pauses and asks, "Why is this spot called Paintball Point?"

"Kids stage paintball wars up on the bluffs," Isobel explains. "My brothers are dying to join in, but my parents don't believe in guns, no matter what they shoot."

"My parents couldn't care less," Vanessa replies. "In fact, they probably wouldn't notice if my little brother bought a hand grenade! They're too busy playing golf with their friends to notice much of anything."

"But they must care about your surfing," Isobel says with surprise. "You said they moved here so you could be closer to the contests and the sponsors."

Vanessa shakes her head. "I said we were moving here. I didn't say it was because of me. My dad joined a law firm in Escondido. I'm just trying to make the best of it."

Suddenly, Isobel has a whole different take on

Vanessa. She isn't the totally together surfer girl Isobel pictured, with a supportive family and clear goals. She's just a confused kid with parents who don't care as much about her as they should.

"I'm sorry," Isobel says. "That sounds rough."

But Vanessa isn't listening. "There's Shane!" she cries, running ahead.

Shane Fox, Rae's former boyfriend, is kneeling in the sand, waxing his board. Shane is in his second year on the pro tour. Two other surfers are with him. Isobel recognizes them from the surf magazines, and from Rae's description. They're Trent Kalesworth and J.J. Bosco, and, like Shane, they're both pros.

"It's about time you showed up," Shane says. "We were getting tired of waiting."

"Good things are worth waiting for," Vanessa says coyly. Then she turns to Isobel. "Isobel, I want you to meet my friends: Shane, Trent, and J.J. Guys, this is Isobel."

Isobel smiles, but inside she feels confused. Wasn't this surf session supposed to be just the two of them? It sounds as if Vanessa invited the guys along, too.

"Aren't you a friend of Rae Perrault?" Shane asks. Isobel nods, and Shane glances at the guys. "She had a big crush on me during the summer, remember?"

"The chick with the strawberry-blonde hair." J.J. nods. "She's on the Edge surf team, right?"

"Yeah, thanks to me. But she read my help as something more, so I had to ditch her."

Isobel stares, too stunned to speak. Shane didn't ditch Rae; *she* dumped *him*! But before she can figure out how to respond, Vanessa says, "Enough talk. Let's surf."

They all grab their boards and head for the water. Isobel, her head still spinning, follows behind. As they reach the water's edge, Vanessa slows down to wait for her.

"Anything I should know about this break?" she asks.

"The wave builds up over a rocky reef," Isobel explains. "It jacks up fast, and there's usually a good drop. Rights are best, but there are some nice lefts, too. Sometimes you can get some killer tubes."

"Got it," Vanessa says. Then she adds, "Hope it's cool that I invited the guys."

"Yeah, I guess," Isobel mutters.

"Good!" Vanessa flashes a smile and squeezes her arm like they're old friends. Then she splashes into the water.

The wind is picking up, fragmenting the waves into short, unpredictable sections. Isobel paddles out and joins the boys in the lineup. But they're too busy talking and joking to notice.

"Goose just got back from Tavarua," Shane is saying. "He said it was all-time, and he's got the scars to prove it."

"That reef can be deadly," Trent agrees. "Remember when *Surfing* took us there for that photo shoot? I didn't think we were going to come out alive."

Isobel listens in awed silence. Tavarua is one of the world's most famous breaks, Goose Takaya is a surfing legend, *Surfing* magazine is one of the bibles of the sport—and here she is sitting in the lineup with people who are intimately acquainted with all three.

"What was it like going on a photo shoot?" she asks. "I mean, did the magazine pay for your plane fare and everything?"

The guys look at her like she's some slimy squid who just swam up. "Duh! Of course they paid for our plane fare," J.J. says.

"Did you see my new bikini?" Vanessa breaks in. "I designed it for Eels."

"I was too busy checking out what was under the bikini," Shane smirks.

"Oh, yeah?" Vanessa shoots back. "Well, check this out."

She takes off on a barreling wave that sucks out and immediately closes on top of her.

"Check this out!" the boys shout, mocking her.

"The wind is making them close out," Isobel remarks. But the boys are too busy jeering at Vanessa even to hear her.

Isobel turns away. So much for her intimate surf session with Vanessa. No one—not even Vanessa—is paying the slightest bit of attention to her. With a dejected sigh, Isobel decides to console herself with a wave. Her instinct is to take a set wave, but she knows that on a day like this, the big barrels close out. So she waits for a small but well-formed grinder and paddles hard.

She drops in, cuts hard, and sails into the tube. She's not thinking about Vanessa or the guys now. She's in the moment, and she's loving it.

Ten barrels later, Vanessa and the guys are still name-dropping, trading quips, and ignoring her. "I have to go to work," she tells them. Actually, she isn't due at her dad's store for another two hours, but she needs an excuse to bail.

The guys look up and nod slightly. But as Isobel paddles into position for her last wave, Vanessa follows her. They take off on the same wave—Isobel goes right, Vanessa goes left—and coast in to the shore together.

"I'm sorry," Vanessa says, as they walk toward their towels, "I shouldn't have invited the guys."

"Well . . ."

"Actually, I mentioned I was coming here, and they sort of invited themselves. Still, I should have told them no." She shrugs. "They can get on a major star trip sometimes. It can get old, I know."

"I liked watching them surf though," Isobel concedes. "They really rip."

"You were ripping, too. Maybe they didn't notice, but I did."

Isobel starts to peel off her wet suit, and Vanessa adds, "I meant to tell you. That bathing suit looks great on you."

Isobel is too surprised to speak. Her suit isn't in the same league as a Vanessa Haddix signature model. In fact, she got it at Ross Dress for Less. Still, she does think it looks pretty good on her, and she's pleased Vanessa noticed. "Thanks," she mutters at last.

Vanessa opens her backpack and offers Isobel a Powerade and a granola bar. "Thanks for coming. Like I said, it's hard making friends in a new town."

Isobel wants to tell Vanessa that shooting the pier, flirting with every boy on the surf team, and bragging about her new Eels bathing suit isn't the best way to do it. But she doesn't know how to begin. So she just says, "I think my friends will accept you once they get to know you better."

"Rae is a hot surfer," Vanessa remarks between sips of her Powerade. "She's on the Edge surf team with Shane, right?"

Isobel nods. "But Shane exaggerated when he said he helped her get on the team. He introduced her to Goose Takaya, that's all. It was her talent that got her there."

Vanessa nods thoughtfully. "Is she planning to go pro?"

"Maybe after she graduates. She promised her mother she wouldn't drop out to join the tour like Shane did."

"And what about Luna? With a mother like Cate Martin, she's definitely got the genes. You think she's serious about a surf career?"

Isobel shrugs. "I don't know. I don't think she knows either. She's too hard on herself, if you ask me. She surfs best when she forgets about her mom's legacy and just charges it."

Vanessa rips open her granola bar. "What about the others? You think there are any future pros in the bunch?"

"Maddie's just in it for the boys and the fun," Isobel says. "She's not really part of our crew. Kanani's an amazing longboarder, but she's into soul-surfing mainly. Cricket is talented, just a little undisciplined." She shrugs. "Kanani and Cricket are the youngest on the school team. They're only fifteen—oh, wait, I just remembered. Cricket is turning sixteen next month."

"Oh, J.J. is going off!" Vanessa cries suddenly, leaping to her feet to watch J.J.'s big backside snap.

But Isobel is barely paying attention. She's thinking about Cricket's birthday. "We're throwing a big surprise party for Cricket's sixteenth, two weeks from tomorrow," she says. "Uh, maybe you could come."

Vanessa turns to her, her eyes full of hope. "You think so?"

Isobel wonders if she spoke too quickly. The girls aren't going to want to invite Vanessa—not the way things stand now. But if Isobel can ease the way, maybe get to know Vanessa better and then convince the girls she isn't really the stuck-up goddess she pretends to be, well, who knows? It might actually work out.

"I think so. I'll have to ask."

Vanessa grabs her surfboard. "I can't watch this any longer. Let's get back out there."

"I have to go, remember?"

"Oh, right. Well, 'bye, Isobel. I'll see you in school on Monday."

Isobel smiles. "Later," she says.

On the way back to the car, Isobel wonders if she'll ever understand Vanessa. One minute she's totally self-absorbed; the next minute she's uncertain, almost shy. But when Isobel remembers their conversation about twins, she has to laugh. Vanessa and she do have a couple of things in common—surfing, and pain-in-the-butt younger siblings!

Who knows? Isobel thinks as she hoists her board onto the roof of her car. *Maybe we* can *be friends.*

9

*H*i! It's Roger."

Isobel can still hear Roger's words ringing in her head, even though his phone call was over an hour ago. In fact, their entire conversation has been repeating in her brain like a CD stuck on replay.

Now, as she drives toward Carson Beach, she runs through it one more time.

"Remember how I told you to follow the surf reports and go where the waves are? Well, a big swell is coming through. How soon can you get to Swami's?"

"Swami's?" she repeats. "You mean in Encinitas? My parents aren't going to let me drive down there."

"Not even for ten-foot surf?"

"Not even!" she exclaims, and then wonders if she should lie to her parents and go anyway. If she doesn't, will Roger give up on her and call someone else?

"All right," he says, "meet me at that break where

you held the surf meet. What's it called—Carson Beach?"

A wave of relief washes over her. "That's it," she says eagerly. "When?"

"I can get there by two, I guess."

"Okay. I'll meet you in the parking lot."

That was it. A simple enough conversation. But it had immediately thrown Isobel into overdrive. First, she'd had to convince her dad to let her ditch work and go surfing. Then she'd had to lie (just a little white one) and say she was meeting the girls at Carson Beach. Okay, no big deal. They'd probably show up there anyway. Finally, she'd spent a good half hour picking out the right bathing suit and sweats, fixing her hair, applying just the right amount of makeup.

Now, fast-forwarding to the present, she pulls into the Carson Beach parking lot, her board on the car and her heart in her throat. Immediately, she spots a vintage VW bus with a new black-and-white paint job. An instant later, Roger steps out from behind it and waves. She feels her temperature rise, just like the first time she saw him. She loves his strong, stocky body—so similar to her own. But she also likes the way his fiery red hair, freckled skin, and pale blue eyes are so different.

"Hi!" he calls as she parks beside him. "Wait 'til you see the surf. It's crankin'!"

"Thanks for calling. This is much more fun than working at my father's store."

"What kind of store is it?"

"Sportswear. Actually, he owns five, but this is the newest. It's the reason we moved out here. It's bigger than the others. More like a discount warehouse than a regular store."

"Does he sell surfboards?"

"Not yet, just wet suits for now. I'm trying to convince him to carry them. What kind of board do you ride?"

"Wave Star," he replies. "How about you?"

"It's an old Yater my parents picked up at a yard sale."

"Sweet," he says, standing on tiptoe to check out the board on the roof of her car. "But it's too small for these waves. Lucky for you I brought a spare."

He takes it down from the roof of his van. "It's a big-wave board. A ten-foot gun."

Isobel can hardly wait to get her hands on it, let alone ride it. She's been checking out big-wave boards on the Web for months. And this one's a beauty—a long, lean, black-and-yellow surfing machine. She runs her hand down the rail. "Awesome!" she breathes.

He grins. "Let's get wet."

They slip into their wet suits and jog to the stairs. At the top, they stop to check out the waves. Only about five surfers are out, and no wonder. It's huge! Isobel stares as a surfer drops down an open face. He looks like an ant sliding down a mountain!

"Have you ever surfed waves this big before?" Roger asks.

She shakes her head.

"Scared?"

"A little," she says honestly.

"No worries. Stick with me, and I'll give you some pointers."

The surf is too big to paddle straight out, so they walk up the beach to a spot that's relatively calm. They wait for a lull between sets, when the surf is at its flattest. Then they paddle out, using steady, powerful strokes.

"Pointer number one," Roger says as they head into deep water. "Study the surf until you find the perfect spot in the lineup for your takeoff." He points to a surfer who is paddling for a wave. "He's too deep. He's going to get hammered."

Sure enough, the wave closes out, and he disappears beneath a swirl of angry whitewater.

"Ouch," Isobel declares with a grimace.

Roger nods. "And don't pick your spot based on where I go. Find some landmarks on the shore or in the water. Then you'll be in the sweet spot whether I'm with you or not."

They paddle into the lineup and just sit there, watching as others take off. Eventually, they figure out the perfect takeoff point. They gaze into shore and line themselves up with some landmarks—just to the right of the stairs, straight out from a tall, drooping pine tree.

"Okay," Roger says, "now we're ready. When you take off, you're going to experience a big drop. Stay focused and don't panic. When you finally touch down, you're going to be roaring across the fastest, bumpiest wave you've ever experienced. Lean hard into your bottom turn, and don't try anything cute. Just hang on and gun it."

With his every word, Isobel feels her throat tightening. She glances over her shoulder at the huge walls of water advancing toward her. Why did she think she wanted to ride big waves? She must have been insane!

"I-I don't think I can do this," she stammers.

"I *know* you can," Roger shoots back. "Isobel, do you know who Flea is?"

She nods impatiently. "Only one of the best big-wave riders of all time."

"Well, Flea said it best: confidence is everything." He looks behind him. "I'm taking this wave. The next one is yours."

Before Isobel can protest, Roger moves into position and paddles as if he's being chased by the devil. A huge wave builds beneath him and, suddenly, he's falling, falling . . . Then he's gone from sight—either riding or getting worked, Isobel can't be sure.

The next wave isn't quite as big, but to Isobel it looks like a skyscraper. Part of her wants to lift into the sky and just fly away—anything to avoid riding this wave. But another part of her—a deep, intense part—wants to do what Roger did. She wants to take the elevator drop and rocket across a wall of water. She wants to surf this wave!

She lines herself up with the tall, drooping pine tree on the bluff and starts paddling. Her heart is pounding so hard, she's sure everyone can hear it. The wave rises under her and she paddles all-out. Then—whoa!—she's falling through space. It lasts only a couple of seconds, but it feels like a lifetime. When at last her board touches down, she crouches low and grabs the rail, desperate not to wipe out.

It works. She's got her balance now, so she leans right into a big bottom turn. Now she's speeding across the wave, bumping over the H_2O equivalent of potholes, concentrating with every ounce of her being on making this wave.

She pulls out before it closes and lets out a scream. She did it! She rode the biggest wave of her life!

Pumped with adrenaline, she speed-paddles back to the lineup. Roger is there waiting for her with a huge grin on his face. "Welcome to the big-wave club!" he calls.

They slap a high five and laugh. "How'd it feel?" he asks.

"Epic! Awesome! Like backcountry snowboarding while being chased by an avalanche. I loved it!"

Roger chuckles. "Yep," he says, "you're hooked."

Five waves later, they're back on the shore. "Can't we just stay out a little longer?" Isobel asks. "I'm not that tired, really."

"Yes, you are. Your arms looked like spaghetti when you paddled for that last wave." He hands her a towel. "Look, I know you want just one more. But it's always better to stop when you've still got some strength in you. It's when you stay out too long that the serious mistakes happen."

"But five waves? That's nothing!"

"I know, but they were the biggest you've ever ridden. Your adrenaline was pumping, and that alone can exhaust you."

"Okay, okay." She looks up. The sky is getting dark, and the wind is picking up. "Looks like a storm is coming in."

He nods. "The same storm that brought these waves." He pulls a Thermos from his backpack, pours a steaming drink, and hands it to Isobel. "It's yerba mate with milk and honey. Try it."

Isobel takes a sip. It's weird, warm, and good. "Yerba what?"

"Yerba mate. It's the national drink of Argentina, I think." He shrugs. "All I know is I tried it at the health food store and I liked it."

She laughs. "I've got PowerBars. Not quite as exotic, but—"

"Sounds good to me!"

They sit side by side in the sand, eating and watching the surf. "So tell me, Isobel, what do you do when you aren't surfing?"

"Go to school, do my homework. Baby-sit my irritating ten-year-old brothers." She hesitates, wondering if she should tell Roger more. "And I . . . I read."

"Oh, me, too. I was a total bookworm as a kid," he says. "Always reading under the covers with a flashlight, that sort of thing."

"I still do that." She laughs. "What do you like to read?"

"Pretty much everything. Travel and adventure books, history, novels."

"I read a lot of novels," she says. "And"—her voice drops to almost a whisper—"poetry."

"I like poetry," he says, totally casual. "Haven't read much really—just the stuff we were assigned in high school. But I always enjoyed it. Don't tell my friends though," he adds with a chuckle. "Real men aren't supposed to like poetry, you know."

"Yeah, right." Should she tell him she writes poetry, too? No, she decides. That's too private. But maybe someday, if they keep surfing together, and getting to know each other, and talking like this . . .

"Man, it's getting cold," he says. "You want to start a fire?"

"Sure," she answers, eager to have an excuse to spend more time with Roger.

"And guess what? I've got marshmallows!" Grinning like a kid, he opens his backpack to show her.

"You really come prepared," she says, giggling.

"I was a Boy Scout. Come on, let's collect some driftwood."

Twenty minutes later, they're sitting side by side in front of a small, crackling fire, toasting marshmallows.

Roger pulls his stick from the flames and gingerly takes a bite of the warm, gooey sweet. "Hmm, perfect!"

He holds it out for her to taste. She takes a nibble and smiles. "Yum!"

"There's some stuck to your lip." He reaches over and touches her lower lip. His finger is so soft, so warm, and, instantly, her lips start to tingle and her head reels.

He brushes away the marshmallow, then pauses, his finger hovering over her lip. "I wish I lived closer," he says, gazing into her eyes. "We could do this every weekend."

"I . . . I'd like that," she whispers.

"You know," he says, "I think we're getting to know each other better." He reaches out and touches her hand, just like he did the day they saw the sea lions. She tenses briefly, but this time she doesn't want to pull away. Then he leans over and softly kisses her.

Isobel closes her eyes. Her pulse is racing; adrenaline is pumping. If there's anything in the world better than dropping in on a big wave, she decides, this has got to be it.

10

*A*nd then," Isobel says, "he kissed me!"

Rae lets out a delighted shriek and squeezes Isobel's hand. "Way to go, girl!"

Isobel giggles, embarrassed but pleased.

Suddenly, there's a knock on the bedroom door. "Are you girls doing your homework?" Mami calls.

"We're just about to start," Isobel promises.

They wait until they hear Mami's footsteps recede down the hallway. "Did you kiss back?" Rae asks.

Isobel reaches over and turns up the volume on the CD player. It's not just Mami she's worried about. When the twins get bored, they like to spy on her. No way she's going to let *them* overhear this conversation!

"I think I did," she tells Rae. "I was sort of stunned." She frowns, suddenly worried. "I hope Roger doesn't think I didn't like it."

"Guys aren't that perceptive," Rae declares. "As long

as you didn't shove him away, I'm sure he assumed you were thrilled."

Isobel laughs, then grows serious. "I really like him, Rae."

"Have you written a poem about him?"

"I've started one."

"Now I know you're serious." She smiles. "Do you want to hear the song?"

This morning in homeroom Rae announced she'd finally finished writing a song using Isobel's poem, "Dropping In." Now she's brought her guitar over to play it.

Isobel nods eagerly and turns off the CD player. "I can't wait."

Rae takes her guitar out of the case and tunes up. She strums a few chords and clears her throat. "I'm still not used to playing in front of people," she says nervously.

"I'm not *people*," Isobel insists. "I'm your friend." She smiles encouragingly. "Go on."

Rae takes a deep breath and starts to play. "*Paddling hard,*" she sings, "*feeling a wall of water rise beneath me. I'm falling, falling into the unknown . . .*"

Isobel listens, enthralled. It's so amazing to hear someone singing her words! And Rae does it so well. The melody she's written is beautiful. The chords are rhythmic and driving, and her alto voice is rich and strong.

"*Someday I'll find that big wave of emotion,*" Rae sings, "*and paddle into it. Half petrified, half exhilarated, I'll ride my heart into the unknown.*"

The last chord hangs in the air. Rae shrugs self-consciously. "It's not very good. Give me a couple more weeks. I'll rewrite it and—"

"What are you talking about?" Isobel cries. "You can't change a note. It's perfect!"

"Seriously?"

"Seriously. I mean, it's like the words were a tiny seed and now, thanks to you, they've become a flower."

Rae looks overwhelmed. "Thanks, Isobel." Then she grins. "Were you thinking about Roger when you wrote the words?"

"I didn't even know Roger then. But that's exactly how I feel when I'm with him—half petrified and half exhilarated. Rae, do you think I'm falling in love?"

Before her friend can answer, Isobel's mother calls, "Telephone for you, *mi hija*."

Isobel picks up the phone beside her bed. "Hello?"

"Hello, Isobel. This is Jamie Johansson. I'm the president of Wave Star Surf Systems."

Jamie Johansson? The famous surfer who won the Pipeline Masters a bunch of times back in the 1980s? She manages a bewildered, "Yes?"

"There's been some very positive buzz about you, Isobel," he continues. "There aren't that many women riding big waves, but from what I hear, you've got the potential to be one of them."

"I-I do?"

"Isobel, Wave Star wants to help you achieve your goals. That's why we'd like to sponsor you."

This can't be happening, Isobel decides. *They must*

have me confused with someone else. "Me?" she asks. "You want to sponsor *me*?"

He chuckles. "You're Isobel Rodriguez, aren't you? Age sixteen, five-foot-six, a junior at Crescent Cove High School?"

"Uh-huh."

"Good, because I'd like you and your parents to come to our offices here in Carlsbad and meet some people. Are you busy next Saturday? There's a writer from *SG Magazine* coming by to interview some of our girls for an article on up-and-coming teen surfers. I'd like them to include you."

Isobel is floating above the room, watching herself talk on the phone. It's totally surreal. Then she realizes Jamie has stopped talking. Is she supposed to say something? "Uh, sure," she mutters.

"Good. Be here at ten o'clock. That way we can get you fitted for a Wave Star wet suit. And we want to show you the new big wave board we've designed. It's called Jawbreaker, and it's going to be in surf shops this Christmas."

"Uh, sure," Isobel repeats.

"See you then. And, Isobel, welcome to the Wave Star family!"

Jamie hangs up, but Isobel just stands there, listening to the dial tone, too shocked to speak.

"Who was that?" Rae asks.

"Huh?"

"I said who was that?"

"Jamie Johansson."

Rae stares at her dubiously. "The surfer?"

"That's what he said, but it must be some kind of prank." She runs to the bedroom door. "Miguel? Toni? Get in here—*now*!"

"They're skateboarding in the driveway," Mami calls.

"Are you sure?"

"I can see them from the window."

Rae walks up behind her and touches her shoulder. "Isobel, what's going on? Who was that?"

Isobel turns slowly. "I told you. Jamie Johansson. He's the president of Wave Star Surf Systems and—" Now it's starting to hit her. This is for real! "—and they want to sponsor me!"

Rae lets out a squeal. "Wave Star wants to sponsor you? Oh, my God, Isobel! Do you realize what this means?"

"That I'm having a psychotic break?"

"Possibly! But if it really was Wave Star, and they really do want to sponsor you . . ." She grabs Isobel by the arm and drags her to the bed. "Sit down. Tell me everything he said, word for word."

Isobel tries, but it's all become hopelessly muddled in her head. All she can remember for sure is that Wave Star wants to sponsor her, and that she's supposed to show up at their offices on Saturday at ten.

"How do you suppose they heard about you?" Rae asks. "You aren't on the ASA contest circuit. In fact, you've never competed in a surf contest in your life, have you?"

Isobel shakes her head. "Only the school meets."

"Well, someone's been watching you, that's for sure. Otherwise, Wave Star wouldn't be interested in you."

Isobel looks at Rae. "Pinch me so I know I'm not dreaming."

Rae giggles and pinches her.

"Yow!"

"Well, you told me to pinch you."

But Isobel isn't screaming about that. "I just remembered the rest of what Jamie Johansson said. "They're going to give me a new wet suit. And they want me to be interviewed for an *SG* article about up-and-coming teen surfers!"

Rae whoops, and the two friends hug each other. Then they slap a high five, and Rae announces triumphantly, "Watch out, world! Isobel Rodriguez has arrived!"

Is it true? Isobel wonders, awestruck. All she knows is that she can't wait to find out.

It's only later, after Rae has gone home, that Isobel realizes she has a huge hurdle ahead of her: she has to convince her parents to agree to the whole Wave Star deal.

Most parents, she decides, would jump at the chance to have their daughter sponsored by a big surf company. But her parents' mantra has always been "School first; snowboarding and surfing second." How are they going to feel about committing their daughter to a schedule of photo shoots, surf clinics, and contests? Not very good, most likely.

That's when it occurs to Isobel how little she really knows about all this sponsorship stuff. Rae is sponsored by Edge SurfWear and is the youngest girl on their surf team. Does Wave Star expect Isobel to join their surf team? Do they even have a surf team? She doesn't know.

Maybe I should call Roger, Isobel thinks.

He was teaching a surf clinic when she met him, so she figures that means he's sponsored. But by what company? She doesn't have a clue.

But there's one thing she does know. Any excuse to call Roger is a good thing. So she looks up his number—or what she supposes is his number—and dials.

"Sorry," says a guy whom she assumes is his roommate. "He's out. Not sure when he'll be back."

Isobel hangs up with a frustrated sigh. Why didn't she ask Jamie Johansson more questions? Because she was too flustered, that's why.

Maybe she should call him back. Or just wait until Saturday and ask him everything then. But what if she takes her parents to the Wave Star offices and they do something totally embarrassing? Maybe chant their "Homework first" mantra, or tell Jamie their daughter is too young to be an up-and-coming surfer, or just say no to the whole thing and walk out.

The thought is so humiliating that Isobel decides not to tell her parents anything about the Wave Star deal until she finds out more herself. Instead, she takes out her homework, intent on answering the extra-credit math problem that she and Rae left unfinished. But all she can think about is Wave Star.

Will they want her to compete in contests? It's a scary thought, since Isobel isn't crazy about competing. Will they want her to travel—like maybe to Hawaii's North Shore? Now *that,* she decides, sounds okay!

Tossing aside her homework, she walks to her bureau and takes out her one piece of Wave Star clothing, a comfy navy blue sweatshirt with the company logo—a curling wave with a shooting star shining above it—across the front. Slipping it over her head, she preens in front of the mirror, imagining she's accepting a first-place Pipeline trophy while fans cheer and call her name. Oh, yeah! This is the life!

Her mother's voice brings her back to reality. "Isobel," she calls, "there's someone here to see you. He says his name is Roger. Do you know him?"

Roger! *Here?* With her heart skittering against her ribs, she throws open the bedroom door and runs past her bewildered mother. Roger is standing in the foyer, a beautiful bouquet of flowers in his hand. And—can it be?—he's wearing the exact same Wave Star sweatshirt Isobel is wearing!

Isobel freezes, suddenly overcome with shyness. But if Roger notices, he doesn't show it. Smiling, he walks toward her and hands her the bouquet. Then he kisses her cheek and exclaims, "Congratulations! Now we're both Wave Star riders!"

11

*I*sobel stares at the flowers, then at Roger. His words are still echoing in her head. *Now we're both Wave Star riders!*

"You mean, you surf for Wave Star, too?" she asks incredulously.

"Sure," he says. "What do you think I was doing at that surf clinic on Carson Beach?"

But of course! Wave Star was one of the sponsors of the clinic. Their name was on the tent. But so were a lot of other company names. He could have been sponsored by Chunky Surf Wax or Bali Boards or . . .

And then a terrible thought hits her. Maybe Wave Star didn't offer to sponsor her because they thought she was a talented up-and-comer. Maybe they did it because Roger asked them to. After all, she's only a beginner. She hasn't won any important contests. And, unlike the female riders featured in the Wave Star ads, she isn't beautiful.

"So what do you think?" Roger asks, breaking into her thoughts. "Are you excited about riding for Wave Star?"

"I . . . I guess so," she answers. "The truth is, I don't exactly know what it means."

"That's part of why I'm here," he says. "Jamie asked me to tell you a little about my experience with Wave Star and, you know, sort of pave the way." He chuckles. "I told him it was your parents who were going to need the hand-holding, not you."

As if on cue, Mami appears behind her. "So, Isobel, aren't you going to introduce me to your friend?"

"Mami, this is Roger Copenhaver," she answers, praying that her mother doesn't say or do anything embarrassing. "Roger, this is my mother."

"*Mucho gusto, Señora Rodriguez*," he says.

"*¿Ah, hablas español?*" Mami asks with surprise. "You speak Spanish?"

"*Un poco.* My father teaches Spanish at UC Irvine."

Mami looks impressed. "Come in and sit down, Roger. Can I get you a drink?"

"*No, gracias.*"

They walk into the immaculate living room. Sometimes Isobel longs to track a little mud on the spotless floor, or maybe rearrange the pillows on the sofa— just toss them every which way. But she knows her mother would have a coronary.

"And how do you know Isobel?" Mami asks, taking a seat on the leather recliner. "Do you go to school together?"

Roger sits on the sofa. "No," he says. "I met her at Carson Beach."

Uh-oh, Isobel thinks. *That sounds like he hit on me. Mami won't like that.* "He was teaching at the beginners' surf clinic," she explains quickly. "Remember— the day of the surf meet?"

She sits beside Roger and puts the bouquet of flowers on the coffee table. Mami eyes it with suspicion. Isobel can guess what's coming next.

"How old are you, Roger?"

"Eighteen."

Isobel sighs. She knows exactly what Mami is thinking. *Too old for Isobel. Besides, he's probably a surf bum with no money and no prospects.*

But it seems Roger can read minds, too. "I go to junior college and work part-time," he says. "I'm planning to major in business."

Now Mami is nodding. "Just like Isobel's father. He owns a chain of sportswear stores."

"Isobel told me," Roger replies. "She's very proud of her father."

Isobel looks at Roger admiringly. He's really racking up the brownie points. And the amazing thing is he doesn't seem to be faking it either. He's just a natural-born parent-pleaser.

"Would you like to stay for dinner, Roger?" Mami asks. "We're not having anything special—just chicken fajitas—but—"

"I love fajitas," he says quickly. "*Gracias.*"

Just then the front door bursts open and the twins barrel in, skateboards in hand. "Will you show us that move you were telling us about?" Toni asks Roger.

"The handstand thing," Miguel adds. "Please?"

Mami smiles at Roger. "I see you have already met my boys."

"Yes, ma'am. We met outside. They were showing me some of their skateboarding moves."

"Sorry," Isobel says, wincing with embarrassment. Her brothers can be such a pain sometimes.

"No worries," Roger says, and amazingly, he seems sincere. "They looked good. But they don't know how to do a hand plant. I said I'd show them." He stands up. "Come on, guys, let's go."

While Mami goes into the kitchen to make dinner, Isobel follows Roger and the twins outside. Next to the driveway there's a small half-pipe, about half as tall as an official one.

"They got it for Christmas," Isobel explains. "I think they'd sleep out here if we let them."

"We're way better skateboarders than you, Isobel," Miguel taunts.

"That's because I never get time to practice," she shoots back. "You're always out here, hogging the pipe."

"Do you skateboard, Isobel?" Roger asks with interest.

"Sure. What else is there to do in Colorado when the snow melts?"

"Show me," he urges.

She borrows Toni's helmet and board and climbs to the top of the half-pipe. Positioning her board on the coping, she leans forward to release her back wheels and drops in. Crouching to gain speed, she shoots up the other side, pauses at the top, and roars down again. Then she busts a frontside air and coasts to a stop.

Roger grins. "You can surf, you can snowboard, you can skateboard. Is there anything you can't do?"

"Plenty," she says lightly, but inside she's glowing.

"Come on," Miguel complains. "You said you'd show us a hand plant."

"Okay, here goes." Roger grabs Miguel's board and hops up on the half-pipe. With lightning speed, he flies down the pipe and up the other side. Reaching down, he grabs a rail with one hand and kicks into a semihandstand on the coping with his other hand. A perfect hand plant!

The boys cheer, and Isobel applauds. "You're good!" she exclaims.

"I used to be," he says as he hops off the board and kicks it into his hand. "But between school, work, and surfing, I hardly have any time to skate anymore."

"Now teach us!" Toni demands.

Roger spends the next few minutes showing the boys how to bust a hand plant. After a few impressive wipeouts, they're starting to get it.

"Papi!" Miguel suddenly shouts. "Look at me!"

Isobel looks up to see her father's car turning into the driveway. He stops and rolls down his window. "Hi, boys!" he calls. "Hello, Isobel." He's smiling pleasantly, but Isobel can see his eyes darting toward Roger, checking him out.

"*Buenas noches,* Señor Rodriguez," Roger says, stepping forward to offer his hand. "*Soy Roger Copenhaver, un amigo de Isobel.*"

Papi shakes his hand. "*Mi gusto,*" he says with a dubious frown. "So tell me—"

"Mami needs your help in the kitchen," Isobel breaks in. "She said to tell you as soon as you got home." A white lie, but maybe it will get Papi out of her hair for a while. Besides, Mami will fill him in on all the details about Roger.

It works! Papi goes inside, and Roger returns to teaching the twins. Isobel sits on the grass and watches him. For a strong, solid guy he's amazingly graceful. And she loves the way he relates to Miguel and Toni, alternately teasing and encouraging them, keeping them laughing as they work at perfecting their new move.

Then Roger turns to smile at her, and her heart flies into her throat. She tries to smile back, but she's so nervous it feels like a grimace. Blushing, she thinks back to her poem. Half petrified, half exhilarated. That's her, all right.

Can this be love? she wonders. It sure feels like it.

"What do you mean Wave Star wants to sponsor Isobel?" Papi asks skeptically. "What is Wave Star? And what exactly do you mean by *sponsor*?"

Isobel pauses, her fork halfway to her lips, and swallows hard. This is it—the moment when Papi starts grilling Roger. Soon Roger will learn how overbearing Isobel's family can be. Then he'll probably dump her and that will be that. No more walks on the beach. No more marshmallow kisses. No more Roger.

But if Roger feels he's under scrutiny, he doesn't show it. "Excellent questions," he says calmly. "Wave Star is a company that makes surfboards and surf gear. Clothing, too. As for sponsorship, that can mean different things. At the lowest level, it might mean giving a hot young rider a free rash guard with the Wave Star logo on it. At the top level, it could mean paying a pro surfer to appear in Wave Star ads and make public appearances."

"And what does it mean in Isobel's case?" Papi asks.

"Wave Star thinks Isobel has the potential to become an accomplished big-wave surfer. They'd like to help her achieve her goal by offering her free gear and free coaching."

Papi puts his chin in his hand and gazes steadily at Roger. "And what do they get in return?"

Roger meets his eye and smiles. "The right to use Isobel's name and photo in their ads. And the promise that she'll use Wave Star gear exclusively."

"And . . . ?"

Roger laughs. "Okay, there is one more thing. There's a new contest being held in Baja this fall—the Salsipuedes Big Wave Open. Wave Star thinks it would be a terrific contest for Isobel to enter. She'd get some valuable big-wave experience, and Wave Star would get excellent exposure."

A big-wave contest? Isobel doesn't know what to think. It sounds exciting, but scary, too. Does she have what it takes to handle something like that? And what about this spot—Salsipuedes? In Spanish, the name means "get out if you can." That's not exactly reassuring!

"Baja?" Mami broods. "That's too far away."

"We're not suggesting she go alone," Roger says quickly. "Jamie Johansson—he's the president of Wave Star—suggested your whole family might like to drive down together. Wave Star would pay for your expenses and reserve a hotel room for you."

"We want to go!" Toni cries.

"Can we, Papi?" Miguel begs. "Please?"

"Hush, *mi hijos*," Mami says. "Eat your dinner."

The boys keep whining while Papi asks more questions, but Isobel isn't listening. She's busy wondering how Roger knows so much about the inner workings of Wave Star. To hear him talk, you'd think he was Jamie Johansson's right-hand man. But as far as Isobel knows, he's just one of their many sponsored riders—and not a famous one either.

Isobel sighs wistfully, imagining herself competing in the Salsipuedes Big Wave Open. Would Wave Star really pay to bring her family along? It seems unlikely. But if it were true, and if she could convince her parents to go . . .

Yeah, right, she thinks. The whole thing is so improbable, it's not even worth thinking about. And yet . . .

Can it be? Papi and Roger are chatting in Spanish and laughing together. And then—miracle of miracles—Papi says, "I have a few questions I want to ask this Jamie Johansson. Saturday, you say? All right, Roger. We'll be there."

"I don't think you realize how amazing you are," Isobel says. Dinner is over, and she and Roger are walking on the hillside behind her house. "I mean, you don't know how uptight and overprotective my father is. When you told him about that Baja contest, I was sure he'd have a stroke. But I think he's actually considering it."

"Good. I'm going to be competing, and it'll be a blast if you're there. Besides, it's a beautiful wave. You're going to love it."

"Let's just hope I don't have to miss any school. My parents will never agree to that."

"One step at a time, Isobel," Roger says reassuringly. "First your parents will meet Jamie. Then they'll see how much fun it is to have their daughter written up in *SG Magazine*."

"Oh, we forgot to tell them about that!" Isobel realizes.

"I didn't want to overwhelm them. Jamie will talk to them about it on Saturday."

They walk on in silence a moment. Then Roger turns to her and says, "I like your parents. It's obvious how much they care about you." He reaches out and caresses her cheek. "I guess it's pretty obvious that I care, too."

Isobel's knees go weak. She wants to tell him she feels the same way, but she doesn't trust her voice. It might come out as a growl or a high-pitched squeak.

"I care about your surfing, too," he continues. "You've got the right stuff. Even Jamie agrees."

Roger's words break the mood. Once again she finds herself wondering why Wave Star wants to sponsor *her*—a total unknown. Did Roger pull some strings?

"Did you tell Jamie Johansson about my surfing?" she asks. "Is that why they're taking a chance on me?"

"I didn't have to," Roger replies. "Jamie was at Carson Beach. He saw you surf."

"He was?" she asks with surprise. "But are you sure—?"

"What? That you're good enough?" He takes her hand and pulls her close. "You're good enough, Isobel," he whispers. "You're *way* good." Then he kisses her.

Isobel isn't thinking about Wave Star now. She isn't conscious of anything except Roger and his sweet, warm lips.

Then suddenly, she hears a giggle. "Isobel and Roger sitting in a tree. K-I-S-S-I-N-G!"

She spins around. Miguel and Toni are hiding in a grove of eucalyptus trees, spying on them. "First comes love," they chant, "then comes marriage, then comes Roger with the baby carriage!"

Roger laughs, but Isobel can only groan. It's so mortifying! How she wishes she could run away to Baja and never return—anything to break free of her embarrassing, pain-in-the-butt family!

12

*L*una Bay at dawn. The sky above the horizon is a pale pink. The ocean is gray and glassy. A convoy of pelicans skim the water, rising and falling with the waves.

Isobel stands on the shore, taking it all in. She loves it here—the wide sand beach, the black, craggy rock that marks the lineup, the graceful waves that undulate toward the shore. It's all so comfortable, so familiar, so safe.

But Isobel longs for more. New beaches with bigger, less predictable waves. New challenges, thrills, and triumphs. And now, it seems, her dream is about to become a reality.

Just yesterday she met Jamie Johansson, toured the Wave Star offices, and was fitted for a Wave Star wet suit. She was interviewed and photographed by *SG Magazine.* And, most amazing of all, her parents actually agreed to drive her down to the Salsipuedes Big Wave Open two weeks from now!

Isobel smiles, remembering the way Jamie Johansson charmed her parents. When he told them he thought school should come first for young surfers, they melted like butter in the noonday sun. And when they found out the Salsipuedes Open was being held over Veterans Day weekend, and that Isobel could attend without missing school, they agreed to take her.

Now they were talking about the trip like it was a school project. The whole family was reading up on the history, culture, and wildlife of the Baja peninsula. Papi was eager to go deep-sea fishing. Mami wanted to show Isobel and the twins the hotel in Rosarito Beach where her parents took her on vacation when she was a child. The twins were hoping to catch some lizards, or maybe even a snake.

With her heart soaring, Isobel steps into the chilly water and paddles out to Black Rock. There's no one out yet, so she has her pick of waves. She snags a waist-high breaker and sails down the line, imagining she's roaring across the face of a double-overhead Baja behemoth.

As she kicks out, she holds up her arms in triumph. "I rule!" she proclaims for all the world to hear.

"Watch your back, Princess," a voice calls, "or someone might knock you off your throne!"

Isobel spins around to find Vanessa wading into the shorebreak. "Hey!" Isobel calls, trying to hide her embarrassment. "I thought I was alone."

"Can't let you have all these waves to yourself, can I?" Vanessa asks, paddling out to join her. "Not that they're exactly challenging. I mean, I could surf this junk in my sleep."

Isobel shrugs. It's true the waves are pretty tame today, but she doesn't like to hear Vanessa put down Luna Bay. It's almost like hearing her put down Luna. "It gets bigger than this, you know."

"So your friends tell me. I'm still waiting." Vanessa takes off on a wave, busts a series of radical cutbacks, and ends with a snapping off-the-lip.

Isobel frowns. Vanessa's I'm-above-all-this attitude is totally infuriating. Still, when she paddles out again, Isobel can't resist sharing her good news. "I've got a sponsor," she announces, "and a boyfriend."

For the first time since paddling out, Vanessa gives Isobel her full attention. "Tell all," she commands.

"Well, Wave Star thinks I have the potential to be a serious big-wave rider. They're sponsoring me, and they're going to send me to a big-wave contest down in Baja—the Salsipuedes Open."

"Sweet. I'll be there, too. And who's the boyfriend?"

"Roger Copenhaver." Just saying his name makes Isobel feel warm all over. "I met him at the first surf meet of the year—back when you were surfing for Santa Barbara High. Do you know him?"

"I sure do," Vanessa says with a meaningful laugh. She gazes at Isobel and nods slowly. "I underestimated you, Isobel. You really know how to play the game."

Isobel frowns. "What do you mean?"

"Flirting with Roger so he'd talk you up to Jamie Johansson. That was smart."

"What are you talking about?"

Vanessa looks irritated. "Don't play dumb, Isobel. Everybody in southern California knows that Roger Copenhaver totally sucks up to Jamie Johnasson. And Jamie falls for it, too."

"I don't get it. Jamie Johansson is the president of Wave Star. Roger is just one of their sponsored riders. How much influence can he have?"

"He's more than that. Roger did an internship at Wave Star when he was still in high school. Now he works part-time as Jamie's assistant."

Isobel is dumbstruck. *Why didn't Roger tell me that?* she wonders. "Still, that doesn't mean I got sponsored because of Roger. I mean, according to him, Jamie saw me at the surf meet and liked my style."

Vanessa laughs. "You think the president of Wave Star goes to high school surf meets? Come on, Isobel. You're smarter than that."

"But why would Roger lie to me? And why would he talk Wave Star into sponsoring me? What's in it for him?"

Vanessa shrugs. "Ask the other four or five girls he's convinced Jamie to sponsor."

Four or five other girls? Isobel can't believe it. She thought Roger liked her, only her. "You don't know what you're talking about," she protests.

Suddenly, Vanessa looks worried. "I thought you had this all planned out, Isobel. But now I'm confused. Do you mean you really don't know about Roger's reputation?"

"What reputation?"

"Everyone knows Roger has brownnosed his way into Jamie Johansson's confidence. They also know he likes to be surrounded by adoring girl surfers, the more the better. So you see how it works? The young up-and-comers flirt with him, hoping he'll put in a good word for them at Wave Star. And Roger eats it up."

"But Roger only cares about me," Isobel says weakly. "He told me so."

But did he say that exactly? she wonders. He said he cares about her, she knows that for sure. But did he promise she was the only one? Her heart sinks when she realizes the answer is no.

"I'm sorry, Isobel," Vanessa says gently. "I didn't mean to burst your bubble."

Isobel shrugs, trying to hold back the tears that threaten to well up in her eyes.

"Come on, girlfriend," Vanessa continues. "Look at the facts. You've only been surfing a little over a year. You haven't won any important contests. You've never had your photo in a surf magazine. And then you think Wave Star wants to sponsor you? Get real!"

Isobel feels a tear slide down her cheek. She quickly runs her wet hand over her face and hopes Vanessa won't notice. "You're right," she says sadly. "I guess I just got caught up in the excitement of it all."

The sun has popped above the horizon and more surfers are paddling out. "It's getting crowded," Vanessa says. "Let's go in. I stopped by Java Jones on the way here and bought some muffins."

They catch a wave and ride it to shore. Vanessa opens her backpack and takes out a bag of blueberry muffins. But the muffin tastes like sand in Isobel's mouth, and the lump in her throat makes it hard to swallow.

"Have you ever thought of wearing your hair short?" Vanessa asks between bites. "I think you'd look cute. My aunt used to be a hairdresser and she taught me a few things. I bet I could give you a great cut."

When Isobel doesn't answer, Vanessa turns to her. "Hey," she says suddenly, "are you crying?"

Mortified, Isobel turns her back to Vanessa and wipes her eyes. Then she feels Vanessa pat her shoulder.

"Isobel, what's wrong?" Vanessa asks. "You're not crying about this whole Wave Star thing, are you?"

Isobel nods.

"Come on, you should be happy. You flirted with Roger; you got sponsored. That's good!"

"But I didn't flirt with him," Isobel says, sniffling. "I swear it!"

"All right, all right. Whatever you did, it worked. Now get out there and do more of it! Spend time with Roger. Compliment him. Throw yourself at him if you have to."

"But—"

"I'll talk to some of the other Wave Star girls and see if I can find out what worked for them. If you can keep Roger happy, there's no telling what he'll do for you. You might get your photo in a surf magazine or some free clothes. Wave Star might even send you to Hawaii to compete. Isobel, you've got to play this for all it's worth!"

"But I don't want to suck up to Roger to get favors," she insists. "If I get noticed, I want it to be because of my surfing."

Vanessa laughs. "Well, that goes without saying. Roger's backing will only take you so far. You've got to prove you deserve it by surfing as well as the best girls out there." She puts her arm around Isobel's shoulders and squeezes gently. "That's going to be the hard part. You don't have the experience that the girls winning the contests have. But you've been lucky so far. Who knows? Maybe you'll be lucky at Salsipuedes."

Isobel swallows hard. "Is it a heavy wave?"

"That's an understatement! It can get as big as twenty feet—maybe bigger. I guess Wave Star is counting on it being smaller for the contest. Otherwise, I don't think they would have signed you up."

Isobel can feel a knot forming in her stomach. What if she isn't good enough to surf Salsipuedes? What if she makes a fool of herself and disappoints everyone at Wave Star? Even worse, what if she takes a nasty wipeout and gets worked over—or even seriously hurt?

"I have to go," she tells Vanessa. "I'm supposed to be at work in a half hour."

"Bad luck. I'm going to spend the day training for Salsipuedes. A little weight training, a little surfing. Then maybe I'll go for a jog later on."

Isobel is starting to feel panicky. She's not ready for a wave like Salsipuedes. She's going to get crushed. With trembling fingers, she gathers up her things and trudges toward her car.

"Give me a ring," Vanessa calls after her. "We'll go surfing. And let me know if you want me to cut your hair."

Isobel straps her board to the roof of her car. Then she gets in and sits there, too miserable to move. But it's not the contest she's thinking about now. It's Roger. It hurts to think that he doesn't love her. But what almost hurts more is knowing that he thinks she doesn't love him. As far as he's concerned, she's just another surf-pro wanna-be, throwing herself at him in the hope he'll help her career.

"And to think he dared to tell me he wasn't into 'all that cutthroat wheeling and dealing,'" she says out loud, trying desperately to transform her unhappiness into anger. "Why, that's exactly what he's into!"

But try as she might, she can't get mad at Roger. She still cares for him too much. The realization makes her eyes fill with tears again. Embarrassed, she starts the car and drives quickly out of the parking lot before anyone—especially Vanessa—can see.

13

*I*sobel and Kanani are lying on Isobel's bed, eating brown-sugar toast and waiting for Luna and Rae to show up so they can plan Cricket's surprise party. Last week they selected the date (the Saturday after Veterans Day) and the place (Crescent Cove Beach Park). Now they just have to work out the details—the food, the decorations, and the music.

"This is delicious!" Kanani exclaims, taking a bite of her toast. "How do you make it?"

"Easy. Just butter a piece of bread. Then add brown sugar and a little cinnamon on top. Put it in the toaster oven until the butter melts. That's it."

"It's the ultimate comfort food," Kanani says with a sigh.

Isobel used to think so, too. When she was little and she skinned her knee, her mother's brown-sugar toast would take away the pain. But not even brown-sugar toast can ease the pain of finding out that Roger doesn't like her.

Or does he? Since her talk with Vanessa last week, Isobel hasn't been sure what to think. Sometimes she wonders if Vanessa might have misread the situation. Sure, Roger probably knows lots of female surfers. But does that mean he's granting them favors in return for their affection? Isobel just doesn't know.

But there's one thing she does know: The very act of doubting Roger has left her paralyzed with indecision. How should she act toward him? If she's sweet and loving, he might think she's sucking up to him. If she's cool and distant, he might think she doesn't care for him anymore.

She's been so anxious that she hasn't had the courage to talk to him, let alone see him. He's called twice, but the first time she bribed Miguel to tell him she wasn't home. The second time, she answered the phone. When she heard his voice, she was so flustered she hung up. When he called back, she didn't answer.

Then yesterday, Jamie Johansson called to tell her he wants Roger to coach her for the contest. "I want you to surf together as much as you can over the next couple of weeks," he said. "Surf the biggest waves you can find. And pay attention to everything Roger tells you. He's a good big-wave surfer, and he'll help you hone your skills."

But Isobel hasn't called Roger. The thought of surfing with him is totally stress producing. She'd probably wipe out on every wave.

If only she could share her worries with someone. Someone who could help her get a perspective on the whole mess. Someone like Kanani, her first and best friend in Crescent Cove.

"Kanani," she begins hesitantly, "I need your help. It's about Roger. You see, Vanessa said . . ."

Soon it's all spilling out—everything Vanessa told her about Roger. "He never told me that he works part-time for Jamie Johansson," she concludes. "And now I'm wondering—is Wave Star sponsoring me because I deserve it, or because Roger pulled some strings?"

Kanani frowns, thinking it over. "Roger is just a part-time assistant. How much pull can he have?"

"Vanessa says he has plenty. And she says he encourages girls to flirt with him in return for favors."

"Did he encourage you?" she asks.

Isobel shrugs. "I didn't think so, but now I'm not sure what to think. I'm just so confused!"

Kanani crosses her legs and leans against the wall. "I don't know what to think either. But I'll tell you one thing. I wouldn't trust anything Vanessa Haddix tells you. That girl is whack."

"No, she's not," Isobel replies. "I mean, sure, she comes on too strong sometimes. But that's because she's in a new town, trying to make a good impression. In private she's totally different."

"Since when do you know so much about Vanessa's private life?" Kanani asks.

Isobel hesitates. "Well . . . we've been hanging out," she admits.

"You and Vanessa?" Kanani asks incredulously. "What for?"

"She asked me to go surfing with her at Paintball Point. You know, sort of show her around. It would have been really mean to say no. Besides, I figured if Vanessa and I got to be tight, it might pave the way for us all to be friends."

Kanani stares at her, a look of disbelief on her pretty face. Just then, the bedroom door opens and Luna and Rae walk in.

"Sorry we're late," Rae says. "I had to help my mother lead a trail ride. Five tourists from New York City, and none of them had ever been on a horse in their lives. It was all I could do not to burst out laughing."

"You've got to try this brown-sugar toast," Kanani announces. "Isobel's mother makes it, and it's melt-in-your-mouth good."

"You sound like a commercial," Luna declares.

"Mrs. Rodriguez's brown-sugar toast!" Kanani says in the perky voice of a TV announcer. "It's a little slice of heaven!" Everyone laughs.

"Mami," Isobel calls down the hall, "can you make more toast?"

Luna grabs Isobel's desk chair and sits on it backward. "So, let's get down to business. We've got a problem with Cricket's surprise party."

"What's wrong?" Isobel and Kanani ask together.

"Well, I sent out the invitations, just like we discussed. At first, I didn't hear from anybody. Then all of a sudden, everybody started to RSVP—and they all said they couldn't come. Turns out Vanessa Haddix is having a party at her house the very same night, and she hired some cutting-edge deejay from L.A. Everybody's going there."

"I think she did it on purpose," Rae says angrily. "Somehow she found out about our party and decided to one-up us with one of her own."

"Vanessa wouldn't do that!" Isobel cries, joining Kanani on the bed.

"How do you know?" Rae asks skeptically.

"Didn't you hear?" Kanani sneers. "Vanessa is Isobel's new best friend."

"What?" Luna and Rae gasp.

Isobel can't believe Kanani is acting so catty. "Look, we've done a couple of things together, that's all. What's the big deal?"

"You and Vanessa have been hanging out?" Luna asks with amazement. "But why?"

"Because she asked me to. Because she's new in town and could use a friend. Because I'm the only one of us who's been even halfway nice to her!"

"I'd be nice to her if she was nice to us," Rae declares. "But all she's done since she got here is try to prove how much better than us she is."

"That's because she's scared," Isobel proclaims. "But she's not like that once you get to know her. Sometimes she's sweet and really vulnerable."

Luna doesn't look convinced. "Vanessa doesn't care about anyone except Vanessa. If she acted nice to you, she must want something."

"Is that so?" Isobel says, her voice rising. "I don't suppose it occurred to you that she might just like me because I'm a friendly, welcoming, nonjudgmental person—unlike the three of you."

"Excuse me," Kanani says, her eyes narrowing. "Who was it who reached out to you when you were new in town and didn't have any friends?"

"So why can't you be that way now?" Isobel pleads.

Kanani ignores the question. "Be honest, Isobel. Did you tell Vanessa about Cricket's surprise party?"

Isobel doesn't know what to say. "I . . . I . . ."

"You did, didn't you?" Kanani cries.

Isobel can't believe her friends are ganging up on her like this. "So what if I did?" she says defensively. "I thought maybe we could invite her. Is that a crime or something?"

"If you wanted to invite her, why didn't you say so?" Rae asks. "Instead you talked to Vanessa behind our backs."

"It wasn't behind your backs," Isobel insists, but deep down she knows it was. Still, she consoles herself, it wasn't because she didn't want to tell. She just wasn't sure her girlfriends would understand. And she was right. They don't.

"This sucks," Rae mutters. "Cricket's surprise party is totally ruined."

Rae doesn't say anything else, but Isobel knows what she's thinking. *And it's all Isobel's fault.*

"Don't blame me," she cries. "I didn't do anything wrong, and neither did Vanessa. If she planned her party for the same night as ours, it was just a coincidence."

"Then call her and ask her to change it," Kanani says.

Isobel tries to imagine calling Vanessa and asking her to change the date of her party. It should be easy, she thinks, but somehow the thought makes her stomach churn. *Could it be that the girls are right?* she wonders. *Could it be that Vanessa is purposely trying to ruin our party?*

But then that would mean the girls *are* right— Vanessa is a self-centered manipulator, and Isobel was a fool to fall for her lies. The possibility is so mortifying that Isobel rejects it immediately. Instead, she jumps to her feet and says, "Vanessa is my friend. If you three don't like it, you can take a hike."

Rae jumps up, too. "That's sounds like a good idea to me," she says in a chilly voice. "Come on, Luna, let's get out of here."

Luna stands up and looks back at Kanani. "You coming, Kanani?"

Kanani looks questioningly at Isobel. Unsure how to respond, Isobel looks away.

Kanani sighs and gets to her feet. "Later, Isobel."

The three girls walk out the door. Isobel can hear them out in the hall, talking to her mother. Then

Mami appears at the door with a plate of brown-sugar toast in her hands. "*¿Qué pasa, mi hija?*" she asks with a perplexed frown. "I made more toast, but your friends said they have to go."

"They forgot they had to be somewhere," Isobel says lamely. "I'll eat it," she adds, forcing a smile.

Mami looks as if she's about to say something more, but Isobel turns away. A second later she hears her mother put down the plate and leave the room. Turning back, Isobel picks up a piece of brown-sugar toast. But the very sight of it makes her feel nauseated.

With a forlorn sigh, she drops the toast and throws herself onto the bed. Tears spill down her cheeks. Nothing can comfort her now.

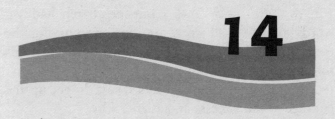

14

*I*sobel lies on her bed, staring at the phone. She's trying to get up the courage to call Vanessa. But so far, she's managed to dial only half the number before hanging up.

Isobel sighs. It's been almost a week since her fight with her girlfriends, and she's never felt so alone. They don't surf with her anymore, or call her on the phone, or stop at her locker to gossip and giggle. When they pass her in the halls, they don't even make eye contact.

And then there's Roger. Yesterday he called again, and Isobel finally spoke to him, but only to tell him she wants to practice for the contest alone. He didn't get it, of course, but what could she say? That she didn't know how to act around him, didn't know what was expected of her, didn't know if he cared for her or not? No, those kinds of worries were just too hard to put into words. So, instead, she told him she had everything under control and she'd see him soon down at Salsipuedes.

Now there's only Vanessa, but she's barely had two words for Isobel all week. Too busy training for the contest and planning her party, she claims. Then this morning it finally occurred to Isobel that she hasn't received an invitation. So she's trying to get up the courage to call Vanessa and ask her why.

Quickly, before she can change her mind, she dials Vanessa's number. It rings twice and then a voice says, "Vanessa here."

"Hi, it's me, Isobel. I was wondering, do you want to go surfing tomorrow morning?"

"Thanks, but no thanks. When a contest is coming up, I like to surf on my own. It helps me focus, I guess."

"I can't believe the contest is only a week away. I hope I don't screw up."

"I hope you don't, too. I checked the online surf report. It's been like double-overhead down there lately. I wouldn't want to see you get hurt."

Isobel winces. Double-overhead! She's never surfed anything that big before!

"So, Vanessa," she begins, taking a breath, "I was wondering . . . uh, I didn't get an invitation to your party yet."

Silence. Then Vanessa says, "Wow, I'm sorry, Isobel. I thought you knew. Roger is coming to my party and . . . well . . . I didn't think you'd feel comfortable being there with him."

Then why did you invite him? Isobel wonders.

But there's another question on her mind as well. Why did Vanessa schedule a party on the same night as Cricket's surprise party? Somehow, she can't bring herself to ask. So she tells herself it must be because Vanessa didn't know the date of Cricket's party. There's no other explanation—at least none she wants to hear.

"So, you want to get together after school?" Isobel says finally. "Maybe grab a drink at Java Jones?"

"I'd like to, Isobel, but between surfing and school and this party, I'm really busy. I'll see you down in Baja though. How are you getting there?"

"I'm driving down with my family."

"Your *family*?" Vanessa snorts a laugh. "Too bad. I'm driving down with the Eels crew."

Isobel pictures a bunch of gorgeous models and surfers, partying their way down the coast. Then she pictures her own version of the trip—sitting in the backseat with her hyper little brothers while her parents drone on about Mexican history. What a drag!

"Gotta go, Isobel," Vanessa says, cutting into her thoughts. "See you at school tomorrow."

Isobel hangs up and reaches for her collection of Billy Collins poems. She leafs through the book, looking for a poem that will express the way she feels inside. Soon she finds one. It's called "Not Touching," and it describes how wrong it feels to be unable to touch the one we love.

". . . still we are not touching," Isobel reads out loud, thinking of Roger. She remembers the feel of his arms around her, his sweet and salty smell, the warmth of his lips.

Her heart aches, and she reaches for her journal. Perhaps writing her own poem will help her make sense of what has happened. But all she can come up with are a few isolated words: pain, loneliness, adrift, abandoned.

She struggles to turn the words into a poem, but nothing comes. Her mind is a total blank. The only thing she can concentrate on is the dull ache in her chest.

Finally, she throws down her pen in frustration. Words won't help her now. She's got to get outside, away from her books, her lonely room, the prying eyes of her family. It's time to go surfing.

Isobel stands at the top of the stairs, zipping up her wet suit as she surveys Carson Beach. The sky is filled with dark rain clouds; the wind is picking up. Out in the ocean, thick, head-high breakers are rolling toward the shore.

Isobel thinks of Salsipuedes, and her insides twist like angry snakes. *Relax,* she tells herself. *This isn't Baja, it's Crescent Cove. You've surfed this wave dozens of times. It's no big deal.*

She descends the stairs and runs into the water. It isn't until she's halfway out that she realizes she forgot to wax her board. Should she go back? While she hesitates, a big set comes in, and she has to fight her way through it.

Why didn't I walk up the beach and paddle out there, the way Roger and I did? she wonders.

She's not thinking straight today. She shakes her head, trying to clear it. But all she can think about is the last time she was here with Roger. They built a fire and toasted marshmallows. He wiped a piece of the sweet, gooey concoction off her lips, and then he kissed her.

A thick wave breaks over Isobel's head. She duck-dives under the chilly water, but she doesn't go low enough. The whitewater catches her board and pulls it out from under her. She pops up and retrieves it just as another wave breaks on her head.

Finally, panting and chilled, she reaches the lineup. There are only a couple of surfers out, some older guys she doesn't know. Normally, she'd join the lineup regardless of who was there, but today she feels anxious and unsure of herself. The guys glance over at her, but she looks away. She doesn't want to chat, doesn't want them checking her out. So she paddles outside and waits there.

Finally, a new set rolls in. The guys take the first couple of waves, but Isobel is too far outside even to consider catching them. Then a massive wave rises behind her. Her heart is racing double-time. Her brain is frozen, but her arms are mechanically paddling as if they weren't connected to her at all.

But wait! What did Roger tell her? She was supposed to study the waves to find the best takeoff spot. She was supposed to line up using a reference point on the beach.

The wave rises up like a surfacing sea monster. Isobel jerks her surfboard back, hoping to let the wave go under her. But it's too late. She's too far into it, and now she's falling . . . falling . . .

Frantically, she rights the surfboard and scrambles into a crouching position. But she's off balance, and the board is a little slippery without its usual fresh coat of wax. She falls through space, her arms flailing. Then she touches down, and, for one glorious instant, she thinks she's still going to be able to make the wave.

A second later, the lip pitches out and smacks her in the back of the head. She's flung off her board like a rag doll. She hits the water with a smack and goes under. Now she's tumbling in the spin cycle, her heart pounding, her lungs burning.

Whack! The board hits her shoulder with the force of a hungry shark. Frightened and hurting, she kicks to the surface. Right behind her, another wave is breaking. A second later, she's pulled underwater again.

Finally, after another anxious interlude in the spin cycle, she manages to find her leash and pull her board back to her. Grimacing with pain, she gets on and lets the waves push her into the shore.

When she finally reaches the shallows, she rolls off into the sand. Her shoulder is throbbing; her breath is coming in ragged gasps. Now she's sure Roger pulled some strings to get her sponsored. Why else would Wave Star have taken a chance on her? She's a terrible surfer. A total loser. She'll probably make a fool of herself at the Salsipuedes Open, she decides. Or worse—get mangled like she did today.

Just when she thinks things can't get any worse, the skies open, and it starts to pour. Wet, cold, and utterly defeated, she trudges up the stairs and goes home.

"Do you remember that hotel we stayed in at Rosarito Beach?" Mami asks Abuelita as she places a ball of dough in the tortilla maker and presses it flat. "It had little bungalows on the beach with thatched roofs."

"*Sí, sí,*" Abuelita answers. She reaches for the tortilla and drops it onto the grill. "You were just a young girl. And your brother Juan wasn't even born yet."

"I remember that place," Abuelo calls from the dining room. "I woke up one morning and found a scorpion in my shoe!"

"*Dios,* how you hollered!" Abuelita exclaims. "They could hear you up and down the beach."

Papi laughs. "Are you sure you don't want to come

with us to Baja? We can rent a van that's big enough for all of us."

"No, no," Abuelo replies. "It's too much driving for such a short stay. We'll go another time. This is a young people's trip."

Isobel looks up from the pot of pinto beans she's stirring. "Maybe we shouldn't go," she says. "It does sound like a lot of driving."

"Don't be silly, *mi hija*," Papi replies. "We know how important surfing is to you. We're happy to take you."

"Oh, I forgot to tell you," Mami pipes up. "Jamie Johansson called today to give us the contest schedule and directions to the hotel. He said the preliminary heats are on Saturday, the semifinals are on Sunday, and the finals are Monday morning."

"We were going to drive down on Friday night," Papi says, "but we won't be able to see anything in the dark. So we've decided to take you kids out of school and leave on Friday morning."

"Hurray!" the twins shout from the living room.

Isobel manages a weak smile.

"On Friday, we thought we'd stop in Tijuana to shop and see some of the attractions—the cultural center and so on," Papi continues. "Then we'll eat lunch in Rosarito Beach, and then . . ."

Papi is going on and on, but Isobel isn't listening. She's thinking about the waves at Salsipuedes. Just a couple of weeks ago she could hardly wait to paddle out in them, but after today . . . well, she just doesn't know.

"Dinner is served!" Abuelita says, carrying platters of carnitas, beans, tortillas, and carrots to the table.

"Boys, turn off the TV and wash your hands," Mami commands.

Isobel takes a seat. Abuelita's carnitas are always delicious, but tonight nothing looks good to her. She picks listlessly at her beans.

"Isobel," Mami says, "I forgot to tell you. Mr. Johansson told me again how excited Wave Star is to be sponsoring you. They think you have a lot of talent."

"We do, too," Papi agrees.

"Yes, *mi nieta*," Abuelita says. "We are all so proud of you."

Isobel forces herself to smile. *I can't let them down,* she tells herself. But deep down, she wishes she could tell them the truth. She's not good enough to surf Salsipuedes. It's only because of Roger's influence that Wave Star is interested. And Roger cares about her only because she's one more groupie to add to his surf harem.

When dinner ends, Abuelita sends Mami, Papi, and Abuelo into the living room to drink their coffee. The twins take their Game Boys and join them. When they're all settled, Abuelita calls Isobel into the kitchen. "You can help me with these dishes," she says. "I'll wash and you dry."

They work in silence for a minute. Then Abuelita says, "I can tell something is wrong, Isobel. Are you going to tell me what it is?"

Isobel looks up, startled. How can Abuelita always read her so well? She sighs. There are so many things she could tell her grandmother—about her wipeout at Carson Beach today, about her friends who dumped her, about her worries over the upcoming contest. But there's something that's troubling her more than all those things.

"Abuelita," she asks, "how do you know when someone likes you for yourself, not just because they want something out of you?"

"Are we talking about a boy?"

Isobel blushes. "Yes."

"Look into his eyes, deep into his eyes. Then listen to your heart. You will know."

Is it really that easy? Isobel can't believe it. But maybe when she sees Roger down in Baja, she'll give it a try. *After all,* she tells herself, *what have I got to lose?*

15

*I*sobel's eyes are as wide as headlights as she walks with her mother and brothers down La Revo, Tijuana's most raucous tourist street. Music blares from nightclubs with names like the Blue Iguana and the Jalapeno Club. Street vendors hawk their wares, and tacky souvenir shops are on every corner.

"Can we ride in the zebra wagon?" Miguel asks.

"That's not a zebra," Isobel scoffs. "It's a donkey with black stripes painted on it."

"Then can we ride in the donkey wagon?" Toni pleads.

"Your father would kill me for spending money on something so foolish," Mami says, clucking her tongue.

But Papi is at one of the budget auto-body shops on Avenida Ocampo, getting a dent hammered out of the car, so Mami finally gives in.

"I'll wait for you," Isobel says.

Mami shakes her head. "No, *mi hija*. I don't want you wandering around by yourself."

Grudgingly, Isobel climbs in the wagon—really a carriage with cracked leather seats. She feels like such a tourist! When the ride ends, Mami insists they all get their photo taken with the donkey.

"Admit it, Isobel," Mami says as they walk away, "that was fun."

"It was dumb," she grumbles. But when Mami tickles her, she giggles and says, "All right, all right! It *was* kind of fun."

Then Isobel spots some beautiful silver earrings in a corner handicraft bazaar. Mami doesn't let her wear anything she considers too big or gaudy, but even she agrees these are pretty. Isobel struts down the street, her new earrings glittering in the sunlight. Then, on a whim, Mami runs back and buys a pair for herself.

Isobel is stunned and happy. "They look good on you, Mami," she says.

Later, Papi picks them up, and they drive to Rosarito Beach. To Mami's delight, the hotel she stayed at as a child is still there. At the hotel restaurant, Isobel and her family devour a lunch of mouthwatering fish tacos.

It isn't until they leave Rosarito Beach and head down the coast that Isobel is reminded why they came to Baja in the first place. On the west side of the toll road, the ocean stretches like an endless blue blanket toward the horizon. Every few miles, Isobel spots a beach break or a point break, all with epic surf, none of them as crowded as the surf spots at home.

If only I were here to soul-surf instead of compete, I'd be in ecstasy, she tells herself.

And then it hits her—maybe if she starts thinking of it that way, the anxiety that's haunting her will disappear. Forget about Vanessa and the other hot surfers who'll be competing against her. Forget Wave Star's expectations. In fact, forget everything except just having fun.

They drive by a killer beach break, and Isobel pictures herself charging it. *I can do this,* she tells herself. *No problem.*

By the time they reach the hotel where Wave Star has reserved a room for them, Isobel is feeling pretty good. They check in, and Papi heads off to look at the golf course. Mami accompanies the boys, who are going stir-crazy from the long drive, to the pool.

Isobel stays in the room to unpack and change into her bathing suit. Then she follows the winding concrete path to the pool. Suddenly, she stops in her tracks and does a double take. Is that Rae and Luna standing outside the hotel restaurant? She moves closer, just in time to see Luna's parents walk out of the restaurant.

What are they doing here? she wonders. But of course, she knows the answer. Rae and Luna must have decided to enter the contest. Isobel's stomach flip-flops like a hooked fish. If she avoids Rae and Luna, her parents will notice and ask what's going on. If she talks to them . . . well, that would be just too awkward and uncomfortable.

Quickly, before Rae, Luna, or Luna's parents can spot her, she runs to the pool. Miguel and Toni are doing cannonballs while Mami watches from the shallow end.

"I can make a bigger splash than Miguel," Toni boasts.

"Liar!" Miguel cries. "Isobel, come watch and tell him he's wrong."

"Okay, okay."

She drops her towel on a nearby chair just as a familiar voice calls out, "Hey, Isobel! So you finally made it."

She spins around to find Vanessa stretched out on a lounge chair, a copy of *SG Magazine* in her lap.

"Hi! When did you get here?"

"Late this morning," Vanessa replies. "I spent the afternoon surfing Salsipuedes, getting a feel for the wave."

Why didn't I think of that? Isobel wonders. Once again, Vanessa is one step ahead of her.

"It was ten-feet, easy," Vanessa continues. "Fast and hollow. Lots of rocks, too. I saw a couple of guys eat it, and it wasn't pretty."

Instantly, all Isobel's confidence vanishes. Her skin feels hot, and her stomach is full of butterflies. Tomorrow's contest isn't about soul-surfing, she realizes, and she can't pretend it is.

Oh, why didn't I let Roger coach me? she frets. *Why didn't I come down early and practice?*

Out of the corner of her eye, Isobel sees Mami approaching. "Mom," she says, "this is Vanessa Haddix. We're on the school surf team together. Vanessa, this is my mom."

Isobel isn't sure why she used the Anglo "Mom" instead of her usual "Mami." Somehow, her real, everyday self—complete with overprotective, Spanglish-speaking parents and loud, squirmy brothers—just doesn't seem good enough for Vanessa.

"Did you drive down with your parents?" Mami asks Vanessa.

"No. I came with the Eels crew—that's one of my sponsors." She turns to Isobel. "We're going into Ensenada tonight. You wanna come along?"

But Isobel knows her parents will never allow it. "No, thanks," she murmurs, silently comparing her trip down the coast with Vanessa's freewheeling journey. Suddenly, her ride in the donkey carriage and her lunch in Rosarito Beach seem hopelessly lame.

"Well, I have to get ready to meet the crew," Vanessa says, standing up. "Nice to meet you, Mrs. Rodriguez." To Isobel she adds, "See you in the surf." Then she gathers up her towel and magazine and walks away.

"Isobel, come *on!*" the twins shout impatiently.

With a sigh, she walks to the edge of the pool and sits down. The boys immediately leap into the water, trying to outdo each other with their cannonballs. But

Isobel can't focus. She's thinking about Salsipuedes. Maybe she should ask her mother to drive her there now. She could paddle out, get the feel of the place, maybe catch a couple of waves.

But the sun is low in the sky, and it's almost dinnertime. She knows what her parents will say. Besides, the truth is she wants to put off her encounter with the hollow, grinding waves of Salsipuedes for as long as she can. So she keeps quiet and watches her brothers, all the while trying to ignore the feeling of dread that's settling in the pit of her stomach.

"Oh, my!" Mami cries as Papi maneuvers over the rocky, uneven dirt road that winds down to Salsipuedes. "The car is going to be filthy!"

"Forget the dirt," Papi says through clenched teeth. "We'll be lucky if we don't break an axle."

"We should have rented a Hummer," Toni declares.

"Whee!" Miguel squeals. "This is fun!"

Sitting behind her father, Isobel looks out the window and says nothing. All she can think about is the waves. How big are they this morning? How fast? How hollow?

Then the car takes one more turn, and they're at the beach. There are about two dozen people standing around, stretching and waxing their surfboards. But where are the waves? She thought Salsipuedes was a point break. All she sees is a gnarly beach break, smashing against the rocks.

Isobel jumps out and immediately spots Roger, standing under a tent, talking to some officials. She stops, paralyzed. Part of her wants to ask him for help, but another part of her wants to avoid him completely.

Before she can decide what to do, he notices her. "Isobel, there you are!" he calls, hurrying over. "The junior women's heats start in a half hour. Here's your jersey." He hands her a yellow rash guard. "I've got some forms for you to fill out, and your parents need to sign a waiver."

He's all business, Isobel tells herself. *I was a fool to think he ever cared about me. To him, I'm just another Wave Star surfer.*

But the thought has barely flashed through her mind when he reaches out and squeezes her arm. "How are you, Isobel? I missed you."

Suddenly, she remembers her grandmother's method for telling if a boy likes you for yourself instead of for what he can get from you. *Look into his eyes, deep into his eyes. Then listen to your heart.*

She gazes up at Roger. His eyes are as blue as the Pacific Ocean and—

"Isobel! Hey, Isobel!" It's Vanessa, and she's waving madly. "Come here. I want you to meet someone."

"You go on," Roger says, looking away. "I need to talk to a few other surfers."

With a sigh, Isobel joins Vanessa. She's standing with a familiar-looking girl with almond-shaped eyes and beautiful black hair. "This is my friend, Kim Ho. She surfs for Eels, too. Did you see the poster of her in *SG* last month?"

Isobel nods, thinking again how totally out of her league this contest is. "Hi, Kim." She pauses, embarrassed. "Listen, I need to ask a question. This is going to sound stupid, but, uh, where are we surfing today?"

Fortunately, Kim doesn't laugh. "The main break is around the point," she says, gesturing toward the cliffs just south of the beach. "There's a channel over there. You paddle out behind the break."

"This is Isobel's first big contest," Vanessa explains. She nudges Isobel and grins. "Time to show Wave Star they didn't make a mistake. Right, girlfriend?"

Isobel's heart sinks. "Right," she mumbles. But can she do it? Right now she doubts it.

"Attention junior women," a guy in a Salsipuedes Open T-shirt calls. "Everyone in the first heat, get your jerseys on and get ready to rumble."

Isobel rushes to get her surfboard—the new ten-foot gun Wave Star gave her. Her parents are huddled beside the car, reading the waiver. "It says this beach has dangerous currents and sharp rocks," Papi says. "Be careful, *mi hija*."

"Don't do anything crazy," Mami says, giving her a hug. "You don't have to prove anything to anybody."

That's what you think, Isobel tells herself. She pulls

on her wet suit and hurries to the water's edge, where five other girls—including Kim Ho—are waiting. Before she has time to think, the air horn sounds, and everyone dashes into the water.

Somewhere behind her she hears Roger shouting, "Charge it, Isobel! Go big!"

Trying to ignore her jackhammering heart and twisting stomach, Isobel paddles into the channel. As she rounds the point, she gets her first good look at Salsipuedes. Her heart leaps into her throat. Ten-foot grinders are racing toward the shore like out-of-control MAC trucks!

Breathing hard, she joins the lineup. Up on the cliff, she can see the judges watching through binoculars. A big wave is rolling in, but she's too scared to take off. Kim Ho snags it and disappears in a splash of spray. Another wave comes. Isobel paddles into position, then panics and pulls back. She loses that wave, too.

Go for it, she tells herself. *Don't wimp out.*

But the set is fading, and the next wave is much smaller than the others. Isobel takes it and—whoa!—she's sailing down the line, hanging on for dear life so she doesn't get pitched over the falls. The wave goes on and on, and, gradually, she begins to relax a little. She tries a few tentative cutbacks and finally bails as the wave approaches the rocks.

She paddles out and tries again, but the same thing happens. When a big wave builds up under her, a panicky feeling grips her chest, and she pulls back. Finally, when the set is almost over, she grabs the last wave and rides it as far as she can.

When the final horn sounds, Isobel paddles slowly in, certain she's blown it. Her family surrounds her, cheering and clapping. But where is Roger? Where is Vanessa? She doesn't see anyone who can give her an objective critique of how she did out there.

Mami leads her to the car and offers her water and PowerBars, but she's too anxious to eat. She has to see the results so she can know the truth. She waits, gnawing on her nails, as the next heat starts, and then the one after that.

And then—at last—the officials post the results. Isobel holds her breath and looks at the list. To her utter amazement, she just barely squeaked by to make the cut.

"I made it to the semis!" she screams, falling into her parents' welcoming arms. "I made it! I made it!"

And then, with a gasp, she realizes what that means. She has to surf Salsipuedes again tomorrow.

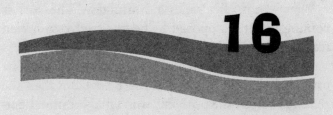

16

"Congratulations!" Vanessa calls as Isobel gets out of the car the next morning. "I see you made it to the semis."

Isobel smiles. At least she has one friend here. Her *former* friends, Rae and Luna, haven't even acknowledged her presence at the contest. Not that she's made any moves to talk to them either. But then why should she? She has nothing to apologize for. They're the ones in the wrong.

"Thanks," she tells Vanessa. "And I saw you scored first in your heat. Sweet!"

"Yeah, and guess what? We're in the same heat today."

Isobel frowns. She can't get too excited about surfing against someone as good as Vanessa. Plus, it's never fun to go up against a friend.

"Rae is in our heat, too," she adds. "And Kim Ho. A pretty impressive lineup, don't you think?"

Isobel nods weakly. She's the least experienced surfer of the four. Great. Just great.

"That's not all," Vanessa continues. "The surf is coming up. It's supposed to be like twelve to fifteen feet for the finals."

Isobel's stomach lurches. Twelve to fifteen feet? She can barely handle what's out there now. But then she reminds herself she probably won't make it into the finals anyway. The thought fills her with equal measures of relief and disappointment.

Isobel suits up and waxes her board, all the while looking around for Roger. But he's nowhere in sight.

Good, she tells herself, but a part of her still longs to see him. She loves everything about him—the way he looks, the sound of his voice, his smell, his touch . . .

No, better not go there. She doesn't want Roger touching her—not if he's treating other up-and-coming surfer girls the same way. She's not interested in a relationship like that.

"Isobel, there you are!"

It's Jamie Johansson. He's a tall man with a shaved head and an imposing stare. Isobel felt intimidated the first time she met him, and she still does. "Hi," she says shyly.

He greets her parents and brothers, and then turns back to her. "Great job yesterday—and without coaching, too. Tell me, Isobel, why didn't you want Roger to coach you? You don't have to do this on your own, you know. Wave Star is here to help you."

How can she explain? "I . . . I was just too busy with my schoolwork," she lies. "My parents say that comes first."

"Yeah, okay," he says skeptically. Then he smiles and pats her on the back. "Go out there and charge it today. Yesterday you were holding back, taking the small stuff. If you want to make it into the finals, you have to go big."

Go big. Just the thought makes her insides buck like a rodeo steer. "Okay," she murmurs. "I'll try."

Soon it's time to make good on her promise. She takes her place at the water's edge along with Vanessa, Rae, and Kim Ho. She glances at Rae, and their eyes meet.

"Good luck," Rae says quietly.

"You, too," Isobel answers. Then she turns to Vanessa to wish her luck, too. But Vanessa is staring straight out at the water with a scowl on her face.

Then the air horn blasts, and Isobel is paddling through the channel once again. The waves are as big as yesterday—maybe even a little bigger—and just as fast. Once again, she takes her place in the lineup. When the first wave comes, she forces herself to ignore her fear and paddle for it.

But Vanessa is paddling, too, even though she doesn't have the inside position. Isobel glances over at her, hoping she'll take the hint and pull out. Instead, she meets Isobel's eye and shouts, "This one's mine!"

Startled, Isobel hesitates. Vanessa jockeys into position and takes off. "Whoo-hoo!" she whoops as she disappears down the face.

Isobel can't believe it. Vanessa snaked her wave! *Although, to be honest,* she tells herself, *I didn't put up much of a fight.*

Frustrated and flustered, Isobel takes the next wave that comes along. Unfortunately, it's the end of the set and once again she's left with the dregs. Still, she pumps it for all it's worth. Then she paddles out, determined to do better next time.

She gets her chance a few minutes later. Another set rolls in while Rae and Kim are still paddling out from their last ride. It's just Vanessa and Isobel in the lineup now. A wave comes up beneath them and Isobel paddles into position. But a second later, Vanessa is beside her.

"This one's mine," she says gruffly.

Isobel is so shocked, she can barely speak. "No, it's not," she squeaks.

"You're out of your league, girl," Vanessa growls. "Pull out or prepare to be thrashed."

Is Vanessa threatening her? Isobel can't believe it. "Vanessa," she begins, "what are you—?"

But Vanessa doesn't wait to hear the end of the question. Taking advantage of Isobel's hesitation, she paddles fast into position and takes off, shouting, "Eat sand, Rodriguez!" as she drops down the face.

Isobel feels as if she's been kicked in the gut. Is this the girl who claimed to be her friend? Friends don't snake your waves, and they don't diss you while they're doing it.

"Are you okay?" a voice asks. Isobel turns to find Rae paddling up beside her. "Why didn't you take that wave?"

"Vanessa beat me to it," she answers, still reeling from the shock.

Rae stares at her incredulously. "She didn't beat you to it. You let her take it. What's going on, Isobel?"

"I . . . I don't know. I thought she was my friend." Isobel's voice trails off. She waits for Rae to tell her off. *That's what you get for trying to befriend Vanessa behind our backs,* she imagines Rae saying.

Instead, Rae cries, "Look at you! You're acting like a whipped puppy. Don't let Vanessa intimidate you like that. You're an awesome surfer, Isobel, but you've got to prove it to the judges. Come on, show them what you've got!"

"But—"

"No buts! Next set that comes through, I want to see you on the biggest wave."

They don't have to wait long. Kim Ho paddles back to the lineup, and Vanessa returns a few minutes later. Soon after that, another set begins to build. Everyone watches the first two waves go by. Kim takes the third wave.

The next wave rears up like a killer whale. "That's yours," Rae shouts at Isobel. "Go for it!"

With her heart in her throat, Isobel starts paddling.

But Vanessa sees her and tries to cut inside. "Leave the big waves for the big girls," she snarls as the wave builds beneath them.

Vanessa's words hurt, and again Isobel hesitates. She just can't believe what she's hearing. How can Vanessa be so mean?

But then Rae's voice rings out behind her. "Don't back down, Isobel! Gun it, girl! Go!"

Before she can change her mind, Isobel goes for it, paddling with all her might. She cuts inside of Vanessa to take possession. The wave is lifting beneath her, exploding from the ocean like an erupting volcano. It's a late takeoff. Can she make it? Or will she be swept over the falls?

Vanessa takes off, too, but Isobel is the one closest to the pocket. She takes the drop and lands it! But Vanessa isn't pulling out. She's still riding, forcing Isobel into the shack. But it works to Isobel's advantage as the wave curls over her and she finds herself flying through a perfect green tube.

When the wave finally spits her out, she's halfway to shore. She busts a couple of power cutbacks and pulls out, her heart soaring. What a ride! She can't believe it!

Suddenly, Vanessa appears beside her. "You'll pay for this, Rodriguez," she growls.

Isobel doesn't answer. What's the point? She knows the truth now. Vanessa isn't her friend. She never was. It's like her girlfriends tried to tell her—Vanessa is only interested in herself. She was nice to Isobel when she needed someone to hang out with, and when she wanted the skinny on the other girls. But when the air horn blew, the truth came out—Vanessa is a liar and a cheat.

After that, Isobel doesn't hold back. She takes her place in the lineup and charges every wave. When the heat ends, she knows she's done her best.

On shore, her family is waiting. "You rock, sis!" Toni shouts.

Miguel hands her a bottle of water, and Mami and Papi hug her tight.

Then, over their shoulders, she sees Roger walking toward her. Instantly, her heart revs into overdrive. But she still doesn't know how to act toward him. Is he a true friend like Rae? Or a snake like Vanessa?

"Isobel, you were on fire!" he exclaims. "I've never seen you surf like that. It was inspiring!"

Isobel unwraps herself from her parents' embrace. "Thanks," she mumbles. Mami and Papi and the boys are walking back to the tent, so she follows them.

Suddenly, she feels a hand on her shoulder. She turns around and finds Roger glaring at her. "What's up with you?" he asks.

"Nothing."

"Don't lie to me. Why haven't you returned my calls? Why didn't you want me to coach you? Why won't you look me in the eye?"

Again, she remembers Abuelita's words. *Look into his eyes, deep into his eyes.*

She forces herself to look at him. "Roger, I . . . I . . ." she says haltingly.

"What? Tell me what's wrong."

She has to force the words out of her mouth. "Do . . . do you like me for who I am? Or do you just want something from me?"

"What do you mean?" he asks with a bewildered expression. "What would I want from you?"

Finally, it all comes pouring out. "Why didn't you tell me you work for Wave Star? Why didn't you say you were Jamie Johansson's assistant?"

"I thought you knew," he answers. "But who cares? What difference does it make?"

"Vanessa said the only reason Wave Star is sponsoring me is because you pulled some strings with Jamie. She said you lied when you told me Jamie was at the surf meet. She said he never comes to rinky-dink contests like that."

"Well, she's right about that." Roger chuckles. "Jamie wasn't at your surf meet."

"But you said he saw me surf at Carson Beach."

"That's right. He was there the day we went surfing together. I asked him to come and take a look at you. He and a couple of other Wave Star execs were sitting up on the bluff."

Isobel's mouth falls open. She'd had no idea anyone was watching her that day. But that still doesn't prove anything. "That's not all Vanessa told me," she admits. "She said you like to flirt with all the up-and-coming young surfer girls. And they flirt back, hoping you'll put in a good word for them with Jamie."

Roger bursts out laughing. "Vanessa Haddix should get a life and stop spreading stupid rumors. Sure, Jamie encourages me to scout for new talent. But I only tell him about legitimate prospects. And I certainly don't make it a practice to flirt with up-and-coming surfer girls!"

"But you flirted with *me*," she points out.

"Is that what you think it was?" he asks. "Isobel, flirting is just fooling around. This is serious. It's the real thing."

Oh, how Isobel wants to believe it's true! But how can she be sure? *Look into his eyes,* Abuelita said. *Deep into his eyes. Then listen to your heart.*

Isobel gazes into Roger's eyes. She can see the love radiating out of them. She can feel it all around her. "It is the real thing," she whispers.

Roger smiles and leans down to kiss her. But just as their lips are about to touch, Mami shouts, "*Mi hija,* they're posting the heat results!"

Isobel and Roger jump away from each other and laugh. Then he grabs her hand, and they run to the judges' tent. With her heart in her throat, Isobel reads the results. Can it be? Vanessa has been disqualified for interference! She's out of the contest—and Isobel is going to the finals!

17

*I*sobel stands on the cliff above Salsipuedes, staring with awe at the waves wrapping around the point. Vanessa was right about one thing—the surf did come up. It's double-overhead!

Can I do it? she wonders anxiously. *Can I go out there and perform?*

Two days ago, she would have said no way. But now she's more experienced and a lot more confident. She's still nervous, but she's no longer completely overwhelmed. She went out there yesterday and charged it on waves almost as big. With luck, she'll be able to do the same thing today.

"Hey, girl!" Rae shouts, stepping up behind her.

Luna is standing beside Rae. "Ready to rip?" she asks.

"I don't know," Isobel answers honestly. "But I know I never could have made it to the finals without you, Rae."

Rae laughs. "What? Because I told you to go for it?

Anybody can say that. It's doing it that's hard. And you did it."

"You helped me more than you realize," Isobel protests. "Vanessa really did a number on my confidence. It took a true friend like you to convince me I could stand up to her."

"Hey, everybody makes mistakes," Luna says.

Isobel nods sadly. "I made a big one. Hanging out with Vanessa behind your back, telling her about Cricket's surprise party—that was stupid of me."

"We shouldn't have come down so hard on you," Rae says with a shrug. "You were just trying to reach out to Vanessa. You didn't write her off like we did. You tried to be nice."

"I love that about you, Isobel," Luna adds. "You're such a good person."

Isobel smiles. "Thanks. But you were right. Vanessa cares *only* about herself. I found that out firsthand."

"Yeah, but you didn't let her get away with it," Rae exclaims. "Good for you."

Down on the beach, an official with a bullhorn announces that there's fifteen minutes until the start of the junior women's finals. "We'd better get going," Luna says.

The three girls scramble down the trail to the beach. Hurrying to the judges' tent, they check the heat list. The finals will consist of three one-on-one heats. Rae is paired with Jo Rezelli, a smooth, fluid surfer. Luna will be up against Sierra Lessinger, a surfer with big, jaw-dropping moves. And Isobel is competing against Kim Ho.

Isobel bites her lip. Kim came in first in their semifinal heat yesterday. And now Isobel has to surf against her. *Will Kim blow me out of the water?* she wonders anxiously. Only time will tell.

Rae's heat is first. Jo Rezelli pulls off some impressive moves, but Rae beats her by one point to win the heat. Next comes Luna. She's a total tube hog, grabbing the hollowest waves and disappearing into the barrel again and again. Sierra Lessinger, on the other hand, has a nasty wipeout and gets caught inside. In the end, Luna smokes her.

Now it's Isobel's turn. As she slips on her jersey, she notices Vanessa standing nearby, watching her. Isobel meets her eye. Vanessa shoots her a nasty look and turns away.

A day ago, Vanessa's evil scowl would have sent Isobel into a tailspin. Today, she just feels sorry for her. But there's no time to worry about Vanessa's problems now. Isobel's got something more important to deal with. The heat is starting, and it's time to surf.

Isobel and Kim paddle into the lineup. The waves are like mountains rearing up out of the ocean. For one long moment, Isobel stares at them, frozen with fear. What if she wipes out like Sierra did? What if she's thrown against the rocks? What if a current pulls her out to sea?

But then she looks up at the cliff. Luna and Rae are there. When they see her looking, they jump up and down, waving and cheering. *I can't let them down,* Isobel tells herself. And what about her parents, and Roger, and Wave Star? They're all counting on her to perform. But most of all, she knows, she can't disappoint herself.

Kim takes off on a grinding ten-footer. When the next wave rolls in, Isobel goes for it. She paddles hard and feels the wave lifting her up, up, up. Then suddenly, she's flying down the face, her board barely touching the water.

Hang on, she tells herself. *Remember what Roger taught you. Stay focused and don't panic.*

She hits the trough and leans into her bottom turn. Now she's tearing across the biggest, bumpiest wave of her life. She doesn't do any fancy maneuvers—she just hangs on for dear life, riding the wave for what feels like forever. Then, when she reaches the rocks, she pulls out and throws her arms in the air. She's stoked!

With powerful strokes, Isobel paddles out and catches another macking wave. But on her third wave, she takes off too late. With a shriek, she flies over the falls. The whitewater churns like a Mixmaster, holding her down so long her lungs feel as if they're going to burst.

When she finally surfaces and gulps in a lungful of precious air, her heart is beating like a rabbit's. She feels panicky, almost hysterical. All she wants to do is get out of the water—*now!*

But she knows if she doesn't catch three waves she'll be out of the running. So she takes a long, slow breath, steadies her nerves, and paddles out again. This time she chooses a smaller wave. But it pays off with a beautiful tube ride and the chance to do some aggressive carving.

By the time the horn sounds to end the heat, Isobel has caught five good waves—including the biggest, fastest wave of her life. She paddles in, so elated she barely notices how exhausted she is. It's only when she staggers out of the water and almost collapses into Roger's arms that she realizes she's totally spent. Her parents help her to the car and she just sits there, surrounded by Rae, Luna, and Roger, too wasted to speak.

Later, when Jamie Johansson comes over to tell her she came in second—right behind Luna and ahead of Kim and Rae—she realizes how little the final standings really mean to her. What matters is that she conquered her fears and rode the biggest waves of her life. Coming in second is just the icing on the cake.

But now, as her family and friends surround her, congratulating her and hugging her tight, that icing tastes pretty sweet.

"Surprise!"

Cricket stands in the doorway of Shoreline Surf Shop, frozen in shock. Just minutes earlier, Luna's parents helped the girls decorate the store with HAPPY BIRTHDAY banners and bunches of balloons. Then the girls hid behind the racks of clothing and waited for Cricket to arrive.

Isobel steps forward carrying the birthday cake she baked with her mother that afternoon. Since Cricket is the ultimate junk food junkie, they decorated it with M&Ms, Reese's Pieces, and Skittles. "Happy birthday!" Isobel exclaims.

Cricket isn't frozen anymore. She's jumping up and down, shrieking and giggling with delight. "You guys!" she babbles. "I almost had a stroke! I can't believe it. I'm just blown away. I'm just . . . let's eat!"

Laughing, everyone gathers around Cricket and hugs her. Isobel places the cake on the checkout counter and pokes sixteen candles into the frosting. Luna's mom lights them, and together they all sing a noisy, off-key rendition of "Happy Birthday."

Cricket's giggling madly, but when it's time to make a wish and blow out the candles, she grows suddenly serious. Isobel has a good idea what Cricket's wishing. Her dad, a legendary Malibu surfer, walked out on Cricket and her mom ten years ago, and they haven't seen him since. But lately, since she's gotten seriously into surfing, Cricket's been trying to find him. Now, as she blows out the candles, Isobel figures Cricket is wishing her dad will come back into her life.

Cricket cuts the cake, and the girls chow down. Then Luna says, "There's still an hour of daylight left. Let's catch some waves!"

Eagerly, the girls head outside and grab their boards, which they left leaning against the front of the shop. Then they jog up Surf Street to Crescent Cove Beach Park and paddle out into the waves of Luna Bay.

It's a perfect session—laid-back and loose. Everyone's laughing and fooling around. Kanani and Isobel ride a couple of waves tandem. Luna and Rae cut in, out and around each other, laughing like maniacs. Cricket takes off on a two-footer and does a handstand on her board!

As the sun sets, the girls build a bonfire and gather around it. Luna's parents show up to grill hamburgers and veggie burgers. As the girls dig into their burgers, Rae says, "I wonder what's happening at Vanessa's party right now."

"Vanessa's having a party tonight?" Cricket asks with surprise.

"It's my fault," Isobel confesses. "I told her about your party, and she immediately planned one for the same night. Nice, huh?"

"Who cares?" Cricket says. "We're here. That's all that matters."

"A toast!" Isobel exclaims, holding up her can of soda. "To friendship!"

"To friendship!" they shout in unison.

"Time for presents," Luna announces. She hands Cricket a small box. Inside is a necklace made out of blue and green beach glass. "I strung it myself," Luna says.

Cricket puts it on. "I love it!"

Kanani gives Cricket some sweet-smelling soap from Hawaii. Rae gives her a T-shirt with one of Luna's silk-screen designs printed across the front.

Now it's Isobel's turn. "I wrote you a poem," she says, taking out a piece of paper. She's written the words in colorful gel pens and drawn swirly designs around it.

"Read it to us," Cricket says.

Isobel feels suddenly bashful. But if she can't share her poems with her best friends, she decides, who *can* she share them with? "Well . . . okay," she says and begins to read.

> *Five friends*
> *Different as the waves,*
> *Similar as grains of sand.*
> *Hanging together, hanging ten,*
> *Cutting up, cutting back,*
> *In our bedrooms, in the green room,*
> *Off the wall, off the lip.*
> *Fighting for possession of the waves.*
> *Fighting for possession of our*
> *Hearts and minds.*
> *Making up, making the wave,*
> *Pulling out, pulling together.*
> *Five friends*
> *Forever.*

There's a long silence, and for a moment Isobel wonders if maybe they hated it. But then she sees the tears in Kanani's eyes, and she knows they didn't.

"It's the best," Cricket whispers.

"I want a copy," Rae says.

"Maybe I can silk-screen it on T-shirts for all of us to wear," Luna suggests.

Isobel can feel her chest swelling with pride. Her friends are amazing!

"I have something to show you guys," Cricket says, reaching for her backpack. "I got it today in the mail. It's a present from my dad." She pulls out a package of surf wax. The paper wrapping has a handwritten note on it. "It says 'Happy birthday, Cricket. I made this stuff myself, and it's way better than what you can get in the stores. Surf on, surfer girl. Love, Dad.'"

"He knows you surf!" Luna exclaims. "That means he's been watching you."

"Or talking to someone who has," Rae adds.

"So why doesn't he call you?" Kanani wonders. "Or better yet, come for a visit."

"I don't know," Cricket replies. "But now I know he still cares about me. And we're going to meet again someday soon. I can feel it."

Isobel hopes she's right. Cricket's been disappointed by her father so many times before. Isobel doesn't want it to happen again.

Suddenly, Isobel hears a noise behind her. An instant later, shadowy figures leap out of the darkness. "*Boo!*"

The girls scream as the kids from the surf team—Jed, Barry, Dwayne, Maddie, Terrell, and Kristian—grab them from behind. Together, they all go tumbling into the sand.

"You idiots!" Luna gasps, laughing. "You scared us half to death."

"Happy birthday, Cricket!" Jed says.

"Happy birthday!" they all shout.

"I thought you guys were at Vanessa's party," Rae says with a suspicious frown.

"We were," Barry admits. "But then we thought, hey, we gotta stop by and say happy birthday to Cricket."

"And play some Frisbee," Terrell adds, producing a glow-in-the-dark Frisbee from behind his back.

Terrell jumps up and flings the Frisbee to Cricket. She tosses it to Kristian, and pretty soon they're all on their feet, laughing and playing. Then Jed grabs a soda can, shakes it up, and sprays cola at Barry. Soon the game has turned into a wild free-for-all, with everyone screaming, running through the shadows, and spraying soda at everyone else. Even Luna's dad joins in.

Isobel shakes up a can and sprays Dr Pepper at Terrell. But at the same moment, Jed blasts her from behind with a can of 7UP. Isobel lets out a shriek. Her hair is soaked, and soda is dripping down her back.

At that very moment, Roger steps out of the shadows and grabs her hand. "I've come to rescue you, fair maiden!" he declares jokingly.

Isobel's surprise soon turns to delight. "Let us fly, brave knight!" she answers with laughter. They run off down the beach, stopping only when the shouts of Isobel's friends have softened to a murmur.

"What are you doing here?" Isobel asks, leaning over to catch her breath.

"Luna invited me," he says, panting. "But I had to work, so I couldn't get here until now."

She stands up and faces him. "I'm glad you're here."

"Me, too. I have so much to tell you. Jamie was totally stoked about your second-place win at Salsipuedes. He says you're an even better big-wave rider than he realized. He wants you to come to his office next week so he can discuss all the plans Wave Star has for you. Isobel, they're talking photo shoots, contests, maybe even a trip to—"

Isobel puts her hand over Roger's lips. "Later. Right now I don't want to talk to Roger Copenhaver, Jamie Johansson's assistant. I want to talk to Roger, my friend."

"I hope I'm more than that to you," he says, taking her hand and kissing it.

Isobel feels as if she's melting inside. "My . . . boyfriend?" she says hesitantly.

He nods. "*Me gustas mucho,* Isobel," he says softly. "I like you a lot."

Her heart is fluttering like a caged bird. "*Yo tambien,* Roger," she answers.

Roger leans close to kiss her. Suddenly, two small figures appear out of the darkness, dancing and chanting, "Roger and Isobel sitting in a tree, K-I-S-S-I-N-G!"

"Miguel! Toni!" Isobel cries. "What are you brats doing here?"

"Don't call your brothers brats," Mami scolds, stepping up behind them. Papi is with her, standing with his hands on his hips. "Luna's parents invited all the mothers and fathers to stop by," Mami explains.

"What are you two kids doing here all by yourselves," Papi asks sternly. "Why aren't you with your friends?"

Isobel groans. Why does her family have to be so overprotective, so smothering, so totally *embarrassing*? It's just not *fair*!

But then Mami says something that completely blows Isobel away. "You were going for a walk on the beach, weren't you, Isobel? Just like Papi and I used to do, long ago back in Mexico. Do you remember our moonlight walks, *mi marido*?"

Papi's frown turns to a smile. "How could I forget, *mi corazón*?"

"Come, boys," Mami says, "let's go find out if there's any cake left. Isobel, Roger, come back soon, all right?"

"All right, Mami," Isobel says with a grateful smile.

Then her family walks away, leaving her alone with Roger. "See what I mean about your parents?" Roger says. "They really love you."

"I love them, too," Isobel says, and she means it with all her heart.

"Now where were we?" Roger asks, taking her in his arms.

Isobel giggles. Then they kiss, and she feels herself falling, falling. It's like dropping in on an epic Salsipuedes grinder—overwhelming, exhilarating, and, oh, so sweet.

WIN A $500 ROXY GIRL SHOPPING SPREE AT ROXY.COM!!!

Luna Bay
a ♥ ROXY GiRL series

One Grand Prize Winner will receive a $500 Gift Certificate redeemable at roxy.com

**ENTER THE ROXY SHOPPING SPREE II SWEEPSTAKES!
Complete this entry form.**

Mail to: **LUNA BAY**
ROXY GIRL II SWEEPSTAKES!
C/O HarperEntertainment
10 East 53rd Street,
New York, NY 10022

No purchase necessary.

Name: _____

Address: _____

City: _____ State: _____ Zip: _____

Phone: _____ Age: _____

🏛 HarperEntertainment
An Imprint of HarperCollins*Publishers*
www.harpercollins.com

♥ **ROXY GiRL**
roxy.com

LUNA BAY
Roxy Shopping Spree II Sweepstakes

OFFICIAL RULES:

1. No purchase necessary

2. To enter complete the official entry form or hand print your name, address, and phone number along with the words "Roxy Shopping Spree II Sweepstakes" on a 3" x 5" card and mail to: HarperEntertainment, 10 E. 53rd Street, New York, NY 10022. Entries must be received by April 1, 2004. Enter as often as you wish, but each entry must be mailed separately. One entry per envelope. Partially completed, illegible, or mechanically reproduced entries will not be accepted. Sponsors are not responsible for lost, late, mutilated, illegible, stolen, postage due, incomplete, or misdirected entries. All entries become the property of HarperCollins and will not be returned.

3. Sweepstakes open to all legal residents of the United States (excluding residents of Colorado and Rhode Island), who are between the ages of eight and sixteen by April 1, 2004 excluding employees and immediate family members of HarperCollins, Roxy and Quiksilver, Inc. and their respective subsidiaries, and affiliates, officers, directors, shareholders, employees, agents, attorneys and other representatives (individually and collectively), and their respective parent companies, affiliates, subsidiaries, advertising, promotion and fulfillments agencies, and the persons with whom each of the above are domiciled. Offer void where prohibited or restricted.

4. Odds of winning depend on total number of entries received. Approximately 100,000 entry forms distributed. All prizes will be awarded. Winner will be randomly drawn on or about April 15, 2004 by representatives of HarperCollins, whose decisions are final. Potential winner will be notified by mail and a parent or guardian of the potential winner will be required to sign and return an affadavit of eligibility and release of liability within 14 days of notification. Failure to return affadavit within time period will disqualify winner and another winner will be chosen. By acceptance of prize, winner consents to the use of his or her name, photographs, likeness, and personal information by HarperCollins, Roxy, and Quiksilver, Inc. for publicity and advertising purposes without further compensation except where prohibited.

5. One (1) Grand Prize Winner will receive a $500 gift certificate redeemable through Roxy.com. HarperCollins reserves the right at its sole discretion to substitute another prize of equal or of greater value in the event prize is unavailable. Approximate retail value $500.00.

6. Only one prize will be awarded per individual, family, or household. Prizes are nontransferable and cannot be sold or redeemed for cash. No cash substitute is available except at the sole discretion of HarperCollins for reasons of prize unavailability. Any federal, state, or local taxes are the responsibility of the winner.

7. Additional terms: By participating, entrants agree a) to the official rules and decisions of the judges which will be final in all respects; and b) to release, discharge, and hold harmless HarperCollins, Roxy, and Quiksilver, Inc. and their affiliates, subsidiaries, and advertising promotion agencies from and against any and all liability or damages associated with acceptance, use, or misuse of any prize received in this sweepstakes.

8. To obtain the name of the winner, please send your request and a self-addressed stamped envelope (Vermont residents may omit return postage) to "Roxy Winners II List" c/o HarperEntertainment, 10 E. 53rd Street, New York, NY 10022.

SPONSOR: HarperCollins Publishers Inc.